BLUE DOG

Also by Louis de Bernières

LOUIS DE BERNIÈRES

BLUE DOG

ILLUSTRATED BY ALAN BAKER

Harvill Secker
LONDON

1 3 5 7 9 10 8 6 4 2

Harvill Secker, an imprint of Vintage,
20 Vauxhall Bridge Road,
London SW1V 2SA

Harvill Secker is part of the Penguin Random House
group of companies whose addresses can be found
at global.penguinrandomhouse.com

Penguin
Random House
UK

Text copyright © Louis de Bernières 2016
Illustrations © Alan Baker 2016
Based on a screenplay by Daniel Taplitz
Executive Producer – Nelson Woss

First published by Harvill Secker in 2016

penguin.co.uk/vintage

A CIP catalogue record for this book is available from the British Library

ISBN 9781910701997

Typeset in Bembo by Palimpsest Book Production Ltd, Falkirk, Stirlingshire
Printed and bound in Great Britain by TJ International Ltd, Padstow, Cornwall

Excerpts from 'Alone in the Evening Shadows' and 'Australia' from
The Drover's Cook & Other Verses, published by Hesperian Press in 1984

Every effort has been made to trace and contact all holders of copyright in
[...] s or errors, the publishers will
[...] rliest opportunity.

[...] to a sustainable future
[...] planet. This book is
[...] cil® certified paper.

CONTENTS

When the sun sets out beyond the range,
O'er scenes of radiant hue,
My thoughts drift through the vanished years
To treasured times with you.

Tom Quilty,
'Alone in the Evening Shadows'

MICK IN THE MIDDLE
OF WOOP WOOP

The dirty old Cessna came down on the landing strip, and bounced. The pilot whooped, and took the aircraft up into the air again. He glanced at the pale little boy beside him, and said, 'Don't be a worry-wart, mate, it's just for fun. You don't get many laughs out here unless you find 'em yourself.'

As the plane banked round for another run, Mick looked out in wonder at the land beneath him. It consisted of brown grass, twisted trees, red rocks and red earth, and pretty much not anything else as far as the eye could see, unless you counted the sea, which sparkled in the distance like a tray of diamonds.

'Everything's red,' said Mick.

'I've brought you to Mars, mate. Thought you'd like some space travel.'

'You can't get to Mars in an aeroplane,' Mick told him, more confidently than he really felt.

'Jeez, you're a sharp one. Might as well be on Mars, though. This is the Pilbara. You've got to be barmy as a bandicoot to live out here. Even the roos and dingos are barmy. Give me Margaret River any day. It's lovely down in Albany. It's stiff bickies you've got to live up here.'

'Port Hedland looked nice,' said Mick.

'Well, it is. Got the best fish and chips in the world. Great place if you like fishing. Caught a shark there once, with a roo steak.'

The plane came down again, and Mick tried not to be frightened. It was scary to see the ground rushing up like that; the plane waggled from side to side as the earth rushed up to meet them, and the thump of landing made his stomach seem to jump up into his throat. He gripped the side of his seat, his knuckles white. After they had slewed to a halt, they sat there for a while until the cloud of red dust that had enveloped them had been given time to disperse. It suddenly seemed very hot in the cockpit.

When the pilot opened the door and told him to clamber out, the heat overcame the boy like a blast from hell. Mick did not know how to react. He had never felt a heat so dense, as if it were made of metal. 'Not so hot today,' the pilot said. 'You're lucky. Sometimes it's like a bloody furnace.'

2

Mick stood on the shimmering earth, and the pilot tossed his blue suitcase down to him, saying, 'Here, mate, catch!' It wasn't a big case, but it was crammed with almost everything that Mick owned, and he fell backwards as it hit his chest.

'Sorry, mate,' said the pilot, as Mick stood up and looked dumbly at the red dust that covered his hands and clothes. 'Better get used to it.'

The pilot came down, and stood against the tailplane, calling over his shoulder, ''Scuse me, mate, just got to shake hands with the unemployed.'

Mick was from a polite family in Sydney, and it filled him with wonder that someone would actually wee in public without embarrassment. He was busting himself, but he was going to wait until the aircraft had gone. When he grew older, and told foreigners that he came from Sydney, he'd add, 'But Sydney isn't really Australia.' This was something he was just beginning to learn as he stood out there in the desert, a city boy of eleven years who felt as if he had lost everything.

The pilot finished, buttoned himself up, and said cheerfully, 'No one to meet you. That's a shame. Don't worry, someone'll be along in two shakes. I'll leave you a bottle of water. And you can have my sandwiches. Bloody Vegemite and cucumber. She knows I don't like it.'

'Why don't you just make your own sandwiches then?' asked Mick sensibly, but the pilot just looked at him as if he was mad, and replied, 'Take my advice, mate, don't get married. You're better off with a dog, and that's the truth.'

Mick sat on his suitcase and watched the plane take off in another plume of dust, and then disappear, the sun glinting on its wings despite its shabbiness. It banked as it turned back towards Port Hedland, waggling its wings in friendly farewell. Mick had liked that strange, humorous, rough-hewn pilot, and the thought struck him that maybe when he grew up he could be a bush pilot too, or a flying doctor.

The noise of the engine faded out in the distance, and Mick realised that he was completely alone. It was slightly strange not to be feeling the vibration and noise of the plane any more. The heat was stunning, and there was nothing he could do but sit there and wait, fighting back the panic and horror of being alone in this vast alien place of spinifex and red-hot rock. He opened his suitcase and took out a shirt to put on his head, because he could feel the sun burning his hair off and parching the skin of his face and lips, and reseated himself on the case. He noticed a ta-ta lizard, nearby, watching him with detachment as it raised one foot then another to dispel the heat. It really did look as though it were waving goodbye.

Today had been the end of a long farewell. It was goodbye to Sydney, for one thing. There had been too many goodbyes. Just a few months ago his dad had died, and he still did not really know why or how. Nobody seemed to want to talk to him about it. They just said, 'You've got to be a brave boy, and make sure your mum's

all right.' He couldn't think of his father as dead, not that tall strong man who used to bowl cricket balls at him, and hold him upside down over the garden pond, and show him how to use a sling so that he could play at David and Goliath by hurling pebbles at a Moreton Bay Pine, and told him absurd stories at night until he could keep his eyes open no longer, and would go to sleep laughing. Mick was still numb from it all, and hadn't been able to cry, even in private. They hadn't let him go to the funeral. He'd only been to visit the grave to take flowers to it, and it had given him nightmares afterwards as he imagined what his father might look like now, six feet under the ground.

It had been no use trying to be strong for his mother, because then, when her own father had died shortly after her husband, she'd cracked up altogether. She was 'being looked after', that's what they told him. When he visited her in the home, she sat by the bed in her nightdress, with crooked lipstick, her hair dishevelled, staring past him through the window, without seeing the lorikeets in the trees or the mynah birds on the sill. When he tried to hug her, she did not react, and when he did as he was told, and kissed her hello and goodbye, her cheek felt cold, and too soft. 'How's Dad?' she'd ask him, and he never knew what to say.

A kind nurse told him that his mother had gone on a sort of holiday, because of all the shock and grief, one dreadful thing after another. It wasn't the kind of holiday where you pack your bags and drive up to Byron Bay, it was the kind where your mind closes down for a while. 'Don't worry, Mick,' said the kind nurse, 'she'll come back. They nearly always do. Just give her a while, and she'll be back. You'll have masses of fun with your rellies out west, I know you will. It'll be quite an adventure.'

This is why he'd flown to Perth in a beautiful big airliner, and finally arrived in the Pilbara in a scruffy Cessna, being looked after all the way by a string of kindly people who'd been detailed to take good care of him. He'd had a bucketload of chocolate bars and boiled sweets, and had only been worried or frightened at take-off and landing. He'd completely run out of interesting things to say about himself.

All this bore down on him as he sat and waited out in the wilderness, completely alone apart from the ta-ta lizard, hotter than he had ever imagined it was possible to be, still benumbed by the rapid changes that had overturned his life.

Mick wondered why his granpa had not come out to meet him. He must have heard the aircraft, surely? He wouldn't just leave his grandson out here to bake in this furnace, would he? He couldn't say he knew his dad's father very well, because he only saw him once or twice a year at most, but he knew him well enough to know that he wasn't irresponsible.

Mick felt like crying, but defeated the impulse. He'd become used to having to be strong. He sat on his case as slowly the heat began to drain from the air, and the sun descended in the west, out over the sea. He wondered if he would have to sleep outdoors, and whether dingos ever attacked humans any bigger than babies. There were many tales of dingos eating babies, but he'd never heard of them eating an eleven-year-old boy. He got up and began to search for rocks that were the right size for throwing, searching among the spinifex, and coming back with them and making a neat pile in front of his suitcase. He came upon the ancient skeleton of a red kangaroo, with morsels of skin still attached to the bones in places, and he wrenched off one of the femurs. It was a lovely, big, heavy bone, and when he sniffed at it, expecting to be disgusted, he found that it hardly smelled at all. All the stink had long been burned off by the sun.

He sat down on his suitcase again and took his pocket knife from his jacket. His father had given it to him the Christmas before he died, saying, 'Here, son, you're old enough for one of these now.' He'd shown Mick how he should always cut away from himself in order to avoid a slip and a cut, and how to sharpen it to a razor's edge, because a blunt knife is far more dangerous than a sharp one. Mick had whittled his dad a paper knife for opening envelopes, and given it to him on his birthday as a way of saying thank you. Now that he'd been entrusted with his own knife, he felt he'd reached a new stage in his maturity. His father had promised him an air rifle when he was thirteen, and that would have been the next stepping stone towards manhood.

Mick held the blade at ninety degrees to the kangaroo bone, and set about scraping off the dried pieces of skin. This had to be a good weapon for bashing dingos on the head, and it might come in useful afterwards too, such as to use as a priest if he ever caught a truly huge fish.

He was so preoccupied with his scraping that he did not hear the hoof steps behind him until the horse snorted, almost down his neck. He leapt to his feet from the surprise and shock, and the horse reared up in the air, his forelegs flailing, and whinnying so wildly that it almost sounded like a scream. Mick did not know afterwards whether he had been too frightened to run, or had instinctively known what was the right thing to do. He raised the femur above his head, and faced the horse.

The horse was coated in thick red dust, and was terribly big, as large as a hunter, and Mick could smell its hot dungy odour and grassy breath. It reared again, and then stood, pawing the ground as if it were about to attack him.

'Good horse,' said Mick. 'Good horse. Steady, boy, steady.' His parents had sometimes taken him riding out on tamed brumbies in the Blue Mountains, so he was not as frightened of horses as he might have been. Even so, he could feel his heart thumping in his chest.

The horse had one eye that was completely clouded over, and he cannot have seen anything at all out of it, apart from whether or not it was night or day, but the other eye was large, intelligent and clear. The horse whinnied, and Mick shook the bone at it. The horse lowered his head and went into a posture that was almost a crouch. Mick saw that its mane was horribly tangled.

A warm voice behind him said, 'You riling up my horse, boy? Don't you go whacking it with that bone, now.'

Mick's grandfather was standing over him, shirt-sleeved, brawny-armed, broad-shouldered and sun-beaten, with a broad bush hat thrust down on his head. This was Ronald Carter, a determined cocky out in a place where no sensible farmer would ever have thought of having a farmstead. He put his hand on Mick's shoulder and said, 'Welcome to the Pilbara. Why on earth didn't you come in after you landed?'

'Come in, Granpa? Where?'

Ronald Carter gestured towards a low mound. 'The bungalow's just there. Over that bump. Don't you remember? I thought you'd just duck up, and then I got tired of waiting, and came out to see what you were up to.'

9

'How am I supposed to remember, Granpa? I was two when I was here the last time.'

'Two? Blimey. You mean it was nine years ago? Sorry, son. I remember now, course you were, just a little ankle biter with a fat face and a gobful of cake. Must have lost track of the time. Goes faster and faster the older you get, and that's a fact. What are all those stones for?'

'Dingos,' replied Mick. 'In case I was here all night. Or forever.'

'Blimey. You're the duck's nuts, you are. You're just like your dad. No flies on you. Is that what the roo bone's for?'

'Yes, Granpa.'

'We'd better get you a hat,' said Ronald. 'I'm pretty sure we've still got one of your dad's from when he was your age. I'll take a look. You can't wear a shirt on your head. Folks'll talk.'

The horse had wandered off, and Mick asked, 'Why's he like that?'

'Willy? He was under a gum tree, got struck by lightning. He's mad as a Pommy lord now. I just don't have the heart to put him down. He's supposed to be locked up in the paddock but he kicks down the fence, or jumps it. He's a bloody Houdini. Do me a favour, will you?'

'What, Granpa?'

'Don't ever let 'im out of the paddock, and if you see him out, come and tell me. That feller's damned dangerous. Give him a chance and he goes out looking for a blue. Don't know how you didn't get kicked.' Ronald picked up Mick's suitcase and slung it across his chest so that it hung at the back of his left shoulder. 'Home, James,' he said. 'Advance and be recognised. It's beer o'clock, the sun's goin' down, and it's time to bog in. Don't forget your boomer bone.'

'Did you ever get struck by lightning, Granpa?'

'Me? No. I got mad without it. You have to be mad to live out here. Wouldn't live anywhere else, though.'

At the top of the mound they stopped and watched the sun grow vast and crimson-orange as it slipped down.

'Granma planted a garden,' said Granpa, 'and all that's left now is the little orange tree. While you're here it's your job to water it, right? Not exactly hard yakka, but you might as well make yourself useful.'

Mick nodded, wondering why his grandad had mentioned the tree, and then he noticed that the sun had turned orange, and was disappearing with a final blaze at the crown. The stars suddenly became more visible.

As the temperature dipped, Ronald picked up the case, sighed, and said, 'Doesn't matter how many times I see it.'

LOOKING FOR BUNYIPS
IN THE MULLA MULLA

Mick knew that there weren't any bunyips in the bush, because everyone knew that they lived in the water, but he humoured his grandfather by pretending to do as he was told, and go out and look for one. Granpa wanted him out of the house because Granpa believed that housebound boys were as unnatural and insane as a vegetarian dog.

Mick went out wearing his father's boyhood hat, and it gave him a strange, melancholy, but satisfying feeling to think that he was walking in his father's footsteps wearing his father's hat, with a notebook and a pencil, to look for snakes, as his father had told him he used to do when he was a boy. In fact, his granpa seemed to be making a point of recapitulating his son's

13

boyhood in the person of his grandson, thinking, perhaps, that it would bring Mick closer to what he had lost, by helping him to understand what it had been like to be his father. He was sleeping in his father's old room, in his father's old truckle bed, on the same knobbly mattress, with the same fine mesh on the window in place of glass.

Perhaps this was why Mick had to sweep the veranda every morning, water the orange tree, and then settle down for an hour or two at the big table to do some schoolwork, because that was what was done in the old days. Today Mick had had to trace a map of the world onto a sheet of foolscap, and colour in the countries, and then work out a horrible problem which was to do with how long it would take to fill up a bath that was simultaneously being emptied at a different rate.

But now he was free. He stopped and tried to talk to Willy, but the horse was in a mad mood again, and reared up, baring his teeth at him. 'I don't care what you think,' said Mick. 'We're going to be friends.'

He went to the top of the mound and detected fresh roo droppings. Then he searched for a particularly noisy cricket that seemed to have set up a sawmill in the rocks, but he couldn't find it. What he particularly wanted to find one day was a dingo skull.

He sat on a rock and looked back down at the homestead. He hadn't explored properly, but he knew the layout already. There was a lovely, white-barked, snappy gum tree in the yard that gave shade to the veranda, and a poinciana tree. There was a large work-shop for making and mending, with a big generator behind it in its own stone hut, with three diesel drums up against the wall of it in the shade of the southern side, where they wouldn't get baked by the sun. It was said that fuel barrels could explode in high summer, and send a great ball of fire into the sky.

There was a row of self-contained huts that his granpa said were the same as the ones that Hamersley Iron built for their miners, and this was where the single men had their accommodation. There was a washhouse and a cookhouse, and a tall shiny water tower made of galvanised steel, with a wind pump on a gantry for filling it with water from the boreholes and the cisterns. Granpa was proud of his cisterns. They collected what little rain there was from the roofs. Sometimes, though, when there was a cyclone, the cisterns filled up to overflowing in seconds. 'Why do you have to have a tower, Granpa?' asked Mick. 'Why can't you just pump it when you need it?'

'Pressure,' answered Granpa, without further explan-ation, leaving Mick unenlightened. On the roof of the bungalow was a large shiny tank that soaked up the sunshine and made enough hot water on its own not to need a boiler. 'Got the idea from a Gyppo,' said Granpa, also without further explanation.

In the near distance Mick could see a small convoy of vehicles, consisting of two motorcycles, a ute, and a bull catcher, approaching the homestead. Behind them they raised a pall of rich red dust. For some reason the sight made him think of his mother, all confused and full of tranquillisers, and he felt a pang of sorrow and homesickness. He was in a male society now, and it was as if the softness in his life had disappeared. Still, it would be fun as well as frightening to be out among these rough-and-ready people. Granpa had promised that he would teach him to ride a horse, and handle the mobs, and then he could go home one day and say with some truth, 'I used to be a jackaroo,' something he could be proud of all his life.

Mick went looking for snakes. He had in his hand Granpa's handbook of Western Australian wildlife, and had mugged up on what was dangerous and what was not. He thought the ideal thing to see first would be a spinifex snake, because they didn't usually kill you. Granpa said, 'Don't bother them and they don't bother you. That's the rule.' Granpa had a rhyme that he made Mick learn. It went:

> You see a snake, you step away,
> You tip your hat and say Good Day,
> Pleased to meet you, how d'you do?
> I'm sorry for disturbing you.

Mick was looking forward to finding a snake to recite it to, but soon the day became too hot and bright, and he lost heart. He came back over the mound, and it was then that he noticed a picture on one of the big slabs of rocks. It had been scratched into the surface, so that it showed white against the buff-coloured rock. It was a snake. Someone had drawn a very good picture of a snake, but they had scraped it instead of painting it. Mick felt there was no point in reciting his rhyme to it.

He found his grandfather spiking some bills at his desk, and said, 'Granpa, I just saw something.'

'Did you now? Sure you had your eyes open?'

'Someone's scraped a picture of a snake onto a rock, over there, on the mound.'

'Oh yeah, that's a petroglyph.'

Mick looked confused, so Granpa repeated, 'A petroglyph. There's thousands of them everywhere if you look hard enough. It's the blackfellas, they've been at it for thousands of years. No idea how old that one is. Just keep your eyes peeled.'

'Why did they do it, Granpa?'

'I was taking a shufty at your schoolbook just now, Mick. You've drawn a dog on the back. Why d'you do that?'

'I felt like it, Granpa.'

Granpa shrugged. 'Well, maybe the blackfellas felt like it.'

'Do they still do it?'

'Dunno, son. Whyn't you go and ask? Pop over to Gurarala. And don't draw on your schoolbooks. Not allowed. I've got cartridge paper if you want it.'

'Sorry, Granpa. Granpa?'

17

'Yes, son?'

'It's my birthday tomorrow.'

'Yeah, I know. You're going to be twelve.'

'D'you think that Mum will phone?'

'I'm sorry, son. I honestly think she won't. Too far gone.'

'Granpa?'

'Yes, son?'

'Can we talk about Dad?'

Granpa sighed. 'It'll only upset you. Better not.'

'Granpa, please.' The pleading expression on Mick's face was hard to resist, so Granpa had to give in reluctantly.

'Well, after supper. We'll have a yabber then. I've got work to do, and I don't want to get myself upset. Or you. How d'you like it, being a sandgroper? All right so far?'

'It's hot.'

'Gets much hotter than this. All right, apart from that?'

'Yes, Granpa, but what about Mum?'

'You've just got to wait, son. I'm your mum and dad now, till you get your mum back. Make the most of it. One day you'll be back in Sydney with the cockroaches, and this'll all be gone.'

That evening Jimmy Umbrella, the Chinese cook, fried up a big lump of meat, with a heap of tomatoes cut in half and done in the same fat. Mick was getting used to the big portions of meat, and managed a bit more at every meal. Granpa would say, 'Eat muscle and it makes muscle,' and if Mick left any on his plate, Granpa would help him out and wolf it down. Mick couldn't take the damper bread, though, and Granpa would say, 'Don't blame you, son, it's daggy stuff,' and wolf that down too. Granpa liked it best when it was fried so that it turned into a puftaloon, instead of being a solid lump.

'Is this corned beef?' asked Mick. 'It's really nice.'

'No, it's a dugong. Got run down by a boat. Seemed a shame to waste it, so I bought some of it, and Jimmy cut it up for the freezer.'

'Dugong?'

'The original mermaid, son.'

'We're eating a mermaid, Granpa?' Mick was both puzzled and shocked, and suddenly the meat didn't taste so good.

'Not the pretty kind that sit on a rock in fairy tales. It's like a bloody great seal. It's bush tucker, son, except it's not from the bush, it's from the briny.'

After supper Granpa took Mick out onto the veranda so that they could sit side by side in the darkness, and then it would be easier to talk. Granpa fetched two stubbies and put them beside his chair. He opened one of them, and it hissed.

'You wanted to talk about your old man,' said Granpa.

'Nobody's told me anything,' said Mick.

'Look, nobody knew how to tell you, so they ducked out of it.'

19

'How to tell me what, Granpa?'

'How he died. Why it happened. I expect that's what you want to know.' Granpa paused, and said, 'You know your dad was a policeman?'

'Yes.'

'Well, he was a special kind of policeman. More like a soldier, if you think about it. He went out and dealt with the real scumbags. Drongos with guns. He copped it in the line of duty, son.'

'Dad was shot?'

'Three times. Didn't stand a chance.'

Mick didn't know what to say.

'I'm sorry they never told you how your dad went down. I told them they should. Your mum should have, but she couldn't cope. Anyway, your dad's a bloody hero, son. He was trying to get to a wounded mate, out in the open. You should be proud. Like I am. If I had to lose a son, that's the way I'd choose.'

He was struggling to speak, and Mick could see his grandfather's eyes glowing in the dark. Mick stood up and went and put his arm around his grandfather's neck, and Granpa put his arm around Mick's waist.

'Let's not talk,' said Granpa, but then he said, 'Losing your mum or your dad is bad enough, mate, but losing one of your kids is even worse. I've tried them both. And I want to tell you something about your mum.'

'My mum?'

'Yeah. Don't give up on her. She's a lovely girl. When your dad brought her here for the first time, we all

20

loved her. Always laughing, always singing, always helping. Terrible soft spot for the animals. We had a sick steer that broke its leg in a fence, and she cried over it. She's sensitive. That's why she couldn't cope with what happened to your dad. Don't let anyone tell you she's a loony. She's just broken, and needs mending.'

That night Mick lay awake listening to the grass-hoppers outside, and the distant lamentation of a dingo. He'd been bitten by sandflies that day, and was itching all over. It had never really occurred to him that his dad had been Granpa's little boy, the same way that he'd been his own father's little boy.

When he finally fell asleep he dreamed about the bunyips, and blackfellas scraping pictures on the rocks, and about his dad, out in the urban jungle, having gunfights with scumbags.

MICK'S PRESENT

On his twelfth birthday, Mick wanted nothing more than a phone call from his mother, but he knew it wasn't going to happen. Granpa said she'd gone bush, was still sedated, and hadn't come back from Fairyland.

He got up early, and went for a walk, because first light is a great time in the Pilbara. He visited the little black pigs in their pen, and snorted at them in reply to their demands for a meal. He knew that Jimmy Umbrella would be along with a bucket later, with the leavings from the kitchen, and later on he'd be back with another bucket to collect the droppings for the vegetable patch.

Mick was accompanied by the cat, a fluffy blue Persian of a variety that you often found round there back then, because somebody in Millstream was breeding them. They weren't practical cats for that kind of heat, but there's nothing a cat likes more than lying around getting too hot. This cat was called Lamington, after the cake, which looked nothing like him at all, because the cake had chocolate on top, with desiccated coconut. Lamington got on well with Mick, and followed him around, winding himself round his legs, and miaowing hoarsely.

Mick was walking out to the corral to visit the mad horse, when he heard a terrible racket being set up in the chicken pen, the sound of panic and mayhem, a cacophony of clucking and squawking. His first thought was that it was a fox, because foxes had somehow found their way across the middle of Australia, all the way from Queensland, in the previous century, and continued to be a pest.

It wasn't a fox, however, it was a very large lizard, whose length was about the height of a man, and in its jaws was a brown chook that it was beating against the ground. It threw the bird violently to the earth, picked it up, and then threw it again.

Lamington bared his teeth and spat. He had met one of these before, and knew to stay out of the reach of its tail. His back arched, and his fur bushed out so that he looked like a big spitting ball of blue fluff.

Mick had not met a lizard like this before, and his first thought was that it must be a crocodile, except that it obviously wasn't. He could have run away, but his instinct was to save the chook, so he grabbed a

24

rake that was leaning up against the fence, and took a swipe at the lizard. It dropped the chook and looked at him with its big liquid eyes, its forked tongue flicking in and out of its mouth. Its throat seemed to inflate as if it had swallowed a cricket ball, and it hissed at him defiantly. It was a handsome beast with beautiful markings that looked very like some Aboriginal patterns that Mick had seen out on the rocks.

There was a moment of stand-off, and then Mick whacked it on the head with the rake, whereupon, with lightning speed, it whipped its tail round and lashed Mick across his legs. It hurt so much that he almost couldn't feel it, and in the second before the pain kicked in, he whacked the lizard again. It went up on hind legs, and ran away so fast that Mick could not believe his eyes. It was faster than any animal he had ever seen before, and a great deal faster than he could ever have hoped to run himself. A hundred yards away it stopped, and reared up on its tail to watch him for a moment before resuming its extraordinary sprint.

Mick stood there with tears gathering in his eyes as the stinging of the lash intensified into what felt like a burn. He blinked, not daring to look down at what the lizard had done to him.

Granpa came hurrying out of the house and said, 'Well, you're a fair dinkum chip off the old block, son. Just like your dad. Never backed off from a blue.'

25

Granpa bent down and looked at the stripe across Mick's legs. 'You're going to have a big welt across there, son. It'll be a blue, black and green one, with a red one down the middle, and yellow bits for decoration. Those things can break a dog's leg.'

Mick did not want to say anything because he knew that if he did, he would cry, and he wanted to be a real man in front of his grandfather. He didn't want to move or walk because he knew it would make the pain even worse.

'That was a perentie, in case you were wondering,' said Granpa. 'Pity you didn't kill it, they're pretty tasty. The blackfellas love 'em.' He went over and picked up the chook. 'This one's a goner,' he said. 'Those things have a poison bite. Better put it out of its misery. Can't even give it to the dogs.'

Mick didn't watch as his grandfather dealt with the dying chicken. 'I think it's going to hurt too much to walk, Granpa,' he said.

'You're gonna have to, son; you've got to come and see your birthday present. Happy birthday, by the way. Many happy returns.'

Mick began to walk against the pain and the stinging, and followed his grandfather very slowly. They went round past the dunny house, and into one of the sheds. There was something covered with a dusty tarpaulin, and Mick knew straight away what it was, because the silhouette it made was unmistakable.

Granpa swept the tarpaulin off, to reveal a motorcycle.

Mick couldn't believe his eyes. He was much too young to have a motorcycle. It wasn't something he'd even got around to aspiring to. It was even way beyond an air rifle. 'Blimey, Granpa,' was all he could say.

'Don't get too excited,' said Granpa. 'This is a model 44 Francis-Barnett. It's thirty years old at the least, and it used to belong to your dad. It's got a Blackburne engine, and it's a four-stroke, and it works on a magneto so you don't need a battery. I thought you'd like it, even if it doesn't work. Not that I know if it works or not.'

'How'm I going to get it to work, Granpa?'

'One of the blackfellas. He's a dab hand. You're gonna take it to bits and put it back together again, because that's how you make an old machine get going, and after you've done that you'll know everything you'll ever need to know about how it works and how to mend it when it conks out in the middle of nowhere.'

Mick looked at the ancient motorcycle. It had a dilapidated single seat, with the stuffing coming out, and a pannier on the back. The tyres were perished and cracked all round the walls. It didn't look as if it would ever go again.

27

'She'll be right,' said Granpa, as if he could read his grandson's mind, 'I've ordered new tyres from Perth. How's that welt coming along?'

Mick looked down at his legs. 'It's bruising up,' he said.

'It's gonna hurt like hell for days,' said Granpa. 'I don't suppose you'll be getting on that bike to try it for size, then.'

As they walked back past the dunny, Mick asked, 'Granpa, what does that rhyme mean? The one in the dunny.'

'What rhyme?'

'The one on the wall. It says, "Don't you sit upon this seat, the bloody crabs can jump six feet."'

'Damn, I forgot that was there. I've seen it so many times I've stopped seeing it.'

'But what does it mean, Granpa? I've looked and there aren't any crabs, and they live in the sea anyway. Why would there be crabs in the dunny?'

'No idea,' said Granpa.

That night Mick sat at the table with his grandfather, waiting for Jimmy Umbrella to bring in his special birthday dinner. He had before him a wooden board, a small hammer, a fork and a pair of stout scissors. Granpa had the same equipment, and two longnecks in front of him.

'I'm sorry your mum didn't ring,' said Granpa. 'I hope you had a good birthday anyway. Apart from being whipped by the lizard.'

28

'Will Mum ever be better?'

'No one can tell, son. We've just got to wait. But I'll tell you one thing. Half of me hopes she won't, because if she does, you'll be leaving. This is like having another go at bringing up your dad. Glory days.'

Mick was pondering this, when Jimmy Umbrella came in triumphantly bearing a huge bowl containing a confusion of bright red creatures that looked as exotic and wondrous as anything from Mars. 'Here's him,' said Jimmy, as he put the bowl down on the table.

'Good on ya, Jimmy,' said Granpa. 'Crayfish from Nuriya reef,' he explained to Mick. 'Thank God for eskies. There's no need to look like a stunned mullet, they're bloody lovely.'

'I don't know how to eat them, Granpa,' said Mick, dubiously.

'Well, I'm going to show you.'

'Do I have to?'

'Yes. If you can face down a perentie, you can learn how to eat a crayfish. But don't try and eat the heads. The cat gets them.'

Afterwards, while Mick surveyed the heap of broken discarded shell, happily emitting streams of small burps as quietly as he could, and feeling that weight of delicious crayfish and melted butter settling in his stomach like a brick, Granpa went to the sideboard and came back with a bottle and a small glass.

He carefully filled it with the golden-brown liquid, swirled it a couple of times, and presented it to Mick, saying, 'You're not allowed to drink it, but you've got to have a sniff. Go on, take a deep one.'

Mick took a long breath from the glass and inhaled a deep, beautiful caramelly smell that suddenly set the back of his nose atingle. His head swam pleasantly for a moment.

Granpa took the glass back from him. 'It's Bundy,' he said. 'It's something to look forward to when you're older, like women, but a lot less trouble. Here's to you, son, and happy birthday.'

Granpa took a delicate swig from the glass, sighed, and said, 'Ah, happiness.'

CYCLONE COMING

Taylor Pete and Mick spent a week taking the motor-cycle apart in the shed. It was so interesting that Mick didn't mind being too hot, and covered with oil and grease, with barked knuckles, and cuts that stung. He was finding out that being a mechanic meant accepting all sorts of unexpected minor injuries, and working in strange and cramped positions. In the end, Mick and Taylor Pete lifted the bike up onto a table to make it easier to work.

Taylor Pete was an Aborigine who'd been born on the station and worked there all his life. He was six foot two, with broad strong shoulders like Granpa's. He had a big bush of hair that was going grey, with a wrecked bush hat crammed on top. When he was younger he had been the best jackaroo on that station,

31

and was still the one who did the final round-ups, collecting in all the cattle that the whitefellas on their motorcycles had missed. He'd bring in a good dozen head from every spot. Taylor still rode a horse when he could, and he went in bare feet, walking on hot sharp rocks that would have made a whitefella wince. His feet were big, scarred and gnarled like two slabs of driftwood.

Taylor Pete was the blackest man that Mick had ever seen. Living in Sydney had given him the impression that blackfellas were like creatures from another planet. He had only ever seen one on television, for this was long before you could find them down at the harbour playing the didgeridoo for tourists. In those days, because their traditional life had become impossible, almost all the blackfellas worked on the stations. Everybody knew they were often better workers than the whitefellas, but they were paid a lot less. The number of blackfellas on a station was a big factor in its sale value, just as important as water. Unfairness was built into the system, but it didn't stop the blackfellas and the whitefellas from getting fond of each other, on account of working side by side in a common enterprise for so much of the time. A lot of white people had some insulting names for Aborigines, and the women might get called 'gins' or 'lubras', and no doubt the Aborigines had some insulting names for the whites too.

Mick had no idea how to relate to a blackfella at

first, but after they'd got as far as removing the pushrods, he'd forgotten most of his fears and doubts. Taylor Pete liked to explain how and why everything on the bike worked, and by the time they'd cleaned up the jets in the carburettor, they were fast friends, and Mick had forgotten that Pete was a blackfella at all.

Taylor Pete also liked to tell Mick things that he knew would surprise and shock him, such as how to solve an Aboriginal dispute. 'Well, mate,' he said. 'You grab a spear each, without a barb, but nice and sharp, and you put one leg forward, and you take it in turns to spear the other bloke's thigh, and then one of them gives up, and you rub the wounds with ashes, and that's it. And that's just the blokes. You should see what the women do.'

'What do the women do?'

'They whack each other over the head with a piece of wood, taking turns, until they've both got mashed-up skulls and one of them gives up, and then you'll never guess what.'

'What?'

'They rub ashes into the bloody mess, and that's it, blue over.'

'Blimey,' said Mick.

'Works for us,' said Taylor Pete. 'Those gins've got thick skulls. And guess what else?'

'What?'

'Some of us blackfellas can go invisible.'

'Invisible?'

33

'You get whitefellas taking photographs, and when they're developed, there's a couple of blackfellas there, in the pictures.' Mick looked dubious, and Taylor Pete said, 'If you don't believe me, ask your grandad.'

When Mick did ask his grandad, he replied, 'Yup, everyone knows that,' but Mick was still not convinced. He forgot to ask Taylor Pete if he knew how to go invisible, and in later years always wished that he had.

The day came when it was time to start up the motorcycle, and Taylor Pete gave a hearty heave to the kick-start. It fired on the third kick, and a great cloud of blue smoke came out of the exhaust as the engine rattled into life. 'Wobba wobba!' shouted Taylor Pete, and he danced in a little circle. 'Wobba wobba! Hey, Micko, we've done it!'

The engine settled down and Taylor Pete kept it revved up with the twist-grip until it was warm. Then he took a long thin screwdriver and made some adjustments to the carburettor. 'We'll keep it running a bit fast until it's settled in. Then we'll slow it down a bit.'

It wasn't easy learning to drive the motorcycle. It was really too big and heavy for a twelve-year-old, and when it fell over, Mick had to run and fetch someone to help him lift it back up. It took him ages to learn to use the clutch with any subtlety, and he crashed into a lot of trees and fences. Often he failed to find the brakes in time, and, when he did, his grip on the lever was not really strong enough. The bike bucked and lurched and wouldn't go round corners, and his legs weren't sufficiently long.

It was at this time that Mick made friends with Stemple. Stemple was a good-looking whitefella city boy in his early twenties, who had gone out into the boondocks full of the spirit of romance, determined never to have to do a job that entailed the wearing of a tie. His idea of being an Australian was to be nut-brown from the sun, with rippling sinews in his forearms, who could swim the length of Cottesloe Beach and give the average shark a good run for its money. Stemple was out in the Pilbara working for Mick's grandad, until such time as something came along and made him realise what his life was for.

Whereas Taylor Pete was keen on getting the bike working, because he loved machinery, he was not so keen on having to ride on it. He was a horseman at heart, and it felt completely wrong to be on a motor-cycle.

Stemple, however, loved motorcycles. There were many of them on the farm for rounding up the cattle and getting about the station, but none of them was a bona fide classic like Mick's Francis-Barnett. When he thought that the old man wasn't looking, he helped Mick learn how to control the bike, and utterly wore himself out by sprinting alongside the machine, inhaling mouthfuls of red dust, shouting instructions over the racket of the engine.

Mick received a great many scrapes and bruises

before the miracle happened, and he became at one with the motorcycle, as a jackaroo does with his horse. He suddenly had the most wonderful freedom, and could go wherever he wanted, but both Granpa and Taylor Pete told him never to go out without a pannikin of water and a bag of tools, and there were indeed times when he had a long walk home. His best day was when an emu came up alongside and challenged him. Emus always love a good race, and Mick lost this one because in the end he couldn't go where the emu went.

He was out on the bike one day when he came across a cluster of graves with aged wooden crosses on them, with white writing. He walked among them wonderingly, reading the epitaphs. They were Granpa's mother and father, and Granma, and there were several little graves with children in them, and Granpa's grandparents. There were folk who must have been great-aunts and -uncles, and cousins. On the crosses were painted the causes of death. 'Fever', 'Gwardar bite', 'Typhus', 'Hanged at Roebourne', 'Killed by a Falling Tree in a Cyclone', 'Drowned at Cossack Fishing', 'Speared'. There was one that read 'Don't Know Why' and another that said 'Got Too Old'. It gave Mick a strange feeling, to think that the bones under the ground here were his relatives, and that without them, he would never have existed. It gave him a sense that everything passes away, and that one day he must too. He was sad that his dad wasn't out here in the family graveyard, but in a neat suburban cemetery in Sydney, and then he thought that he was here in his place, having ridden out on his dad's old Francis-Barnett. 'Maybe one day I'll be out here too,' he thought.

That night he asked, 'Granpa, when I'm dead, can I go in the graveyard too?'

'Up to you,' replied Granpa. 'If we still own the place. It'll be good to have the company.'

'If we still own the place?'

'Everything's changed, son. We arrived here in big carts drawn by bullocks, and everyone called my grandad Bullocky Bob. All our stuff came from Freo in sailing boats. We lived off cans of Libby's. Even the spuds were canned. We ate corned beef that came out swimming in melted fat. And you couldn't get bum nuts 'cause there weren't any chooks to lay 'em. No moo juice, and butter wasn't butter, it was warm grease. The pearling beaches were knee-deep in bottles and tins. And we had camels. Now we've got highways and planes, and Karratha Station's ruined. Soon we'll all be gone.'

'Karratha Station?'

'Karratha means "soft country". It was the best station round here. The mining company put a railway through the middle of it, and then they bought it. Two years ago. It was bloody impossible. The miners came out and speared the sheep for their bloody barbecues, and the gates got left open, and the company wouldn't pay compensation. They're building a town on the best paddock. Soon there'll be no more planting up with birdwood and baffle grass, no more moving the mobs from one paddock to another to save the grass.'

'But why would we have to leave, Granpa?'

'Things come and go, son. This place was full of blackfellas once, roaming about, living off what there was. Then it was gold miners until the gold ran out, and pearlers until they moved to Broome. There were folk who set up a turtle-soup factory in Cossack. Even made their own tins. Now it's our turn to fade out. Your dad didn't stay, even though he loved it. When the stations have gone, this'll all turn back to desert like it was before. Desert with iron mines. And one day there'll be something better than iron, and that'll go too.'

Mick didn't know what to say, but his grandfather put his hand on his shoulder and said, 'The important thing, son, is that we lived as we wanted to, and after us, they'll live as they want, and it's not much to do with us, and we'll be under the ground and not giving a stuff. How's the bike going?'

'It's great, Granpa. Stemple's taught me everything, I think. I haven't fallen off for ages.'

'Well, your dad enjoyed it. You know what? One day you're going to take a ride on Blind Willy. Prove yourself a man. We'll start you off on an ordinary horse. Taylor Pete's going to teach you.'

'What's for supper tonight?' asked Mick, adroitly changing the subject.

'Garfish. You'll love it. It's got green bones. By the

way, there's a cyclone coming. The glass just dropped like a bride's knickers. I mean, like a bloody stone. We've got about three hours.'

GREEN BONES

Mick and Granpa stood on the veranda and watched the weathervane spin on the water tower. A small whirl-wind of dark red dust whipped up from the middle of the yard, and spiralled into the sky. Granpa was both calm and worried; worried because there was bound to be damage, and calm because he had been through this so many times before, and had become a fatalist.

Ever since the glass had dropped, Granpa and the men had been rushing from one thing to another, stowing it away or tying it down. Even the henhouse had a chain over it, attached to two concrete blocks. They had shut down the generators, but about the mobs and the cattle they had been able to do very little. Most would survive.

Mick had had some fun in the past, swinging from

41

the chains that held down the buildings, and shinning up them, upside down, sailor-fashion, but it was only now that he fully appreciated why they were there. Granpa said they were attached to railway tracks buried in concrete six feet below ground. The homestead had chains, and so did all the sheds, and anything loose had been brought indoors. His motorcycle was roped through the frame to the base of the water tower.

Granpa said, 'Granma used to have a lovely garden here. It was all zinnias and petunias, and sweet peas and sunflowers, and bougainvillea. She spent hours watering. Then it all got wrecked in a cyclone, and now there's only the orange tree left. I never did have the heart to start another one. That's why we only do veg.'

'I don't really remember Granma,' said Mick.

'That was the one thing she regretted about going early,' replied Granpa. 'She said, "Mick won't remember me."'

A violent gust almost hurled them back against the wall, and Granpa said, 'Time to go indoors and settle down for the blast. Welcome to your first cyclone, son.'

Granpa told Mick to go and sit under the kitchen table, but he sat himself in his usual place at the head of it. In front of him he set his bottle of Bundy, and a small glass. He fetched two hurricane lamps from the cupboard, topped them up with paraffin, and lit them with a match.

Outside the storm started its roaring and howling, and the house seemed to amplify it, like the soundbox of a guitar. Sheets of rain began to hammer at the house sideways, too loudly for them to hear the rattling of the shutters. There were noises that clanged like explosions, and Granpa, as if reading Mick's thoughts, leaned down and said, 'This is what it's like being bombed.'

'Are we going to die?'

'Prob'ly not. Just try and enjoy it, mate. This is where you find out that the world can do without you.'

For Mick, the worst thing was having to imagine what was happening outside. There was no question of going out to take a look, or even trying to peep out of the window. He sat, hugging his knees, and endured the howling, and screaming, the bangs, the crash of sheets of water against the house. He needed to cry but did not want to in case Granpa would think him weak. He began to shiver with fear. Granpa bent down and looked at him.

Mick saw the table begin to move, and at first he thought the storm was lifting the house, but then he realised that his grandfather was moving it up against the wall. Granpa fetched a couple of cushions and crawled in under the table with him, settling his backside on a cushion, and leaning against the wall. 'Thought you might like some company,' he said, and put his arm round Mick's shoulder. Granpa smelled of sweat and Bundy and horses, but above all he seemed to smell of indomitable strength.

'Don't worry, son,' he said. 'You get a half-hour break. You get eight hours from the north-west, and eight hours from the south-east, and then you wander out and tidy up.'

Granpa kept Mick calm by reciting him the poems that he remembered from *The Drover's Cook*, starting with 'Australia'.

> Come all you fervent democrats,
> Prepare to strike with force
> Against our swarming enemies,
> To change their mind and course …

When he finished it, he said, 'I reckon these cyclones are pretty fervent democrats. They pick on all of us just the same.'

Granpa calmly went and fetched the little book of Tom Quilty's rhymes, and they took turns to read them to each other under the table. Mick did not understand 'Rum and Religion', or very many of the others, either, but he enjoyed the occasionally stilted rhythms and the unusual topics, and the sheer silliness of poems like 'Miss Underwood's Cake'.

It was just as Granpa had predicted. After eight hours of that infernal screaming, bass booming, and slashing and banging, there was a sudden lull, and the two went out onto the veranda. The whole yard was covered in wreckage; timbers, sheets of corrugated iron, shredded tarpaulin, vegetation. The beautiful poinciana tree lay on its side, all its leaves ripped off, its branches snapped into ragged stumps. Never again would it flower at

Christmas. At least Granma's orange tree was still standing, albeit with the leaves stripped.

'Bit of a dog's breakfast, but not too bad,' said Granpa. 'Go and see if your bike's all right.'

It was all right, but covered with unrecognisable shreds of everything under the sun.

When Mick came back to the house Granpa said, 'The worst one was 1945. At Karratha Station the river broke its banks and brought in sand a yard deep. They lost fifteen thousand sheep, and they found their horses and cattle hanging on fences, and hanging out of trees. There was twenty inches of rain. Here it was almost as bad. It took the roof off the house and smashed the water tower.

'And you know what? Afterwards we found a wheel-barrow up against the wall that no one'd ever seen before. A bit bashed up, but brand new. And out at the graves there was a nice little sailing boat with the mast snapped off. Must have been rolled there for bloody miles. Never found out who it belonged to. And we lost our rooster and found another one, even better.'

The next phase kicked in with a vast wall of dust advancing on them across the paddock, so they sped back indoors. Granpa cooked the garfish on a Primus, with potatoes and onions and a can of peas. 'It's not as good as Jimmy Umbrella's,' said Granpa, 'but it'll have to do. I'm not much of a cook. Might be a chew and spew. Jimmy'll be hiding up if he's got any sense.'

'Why does he always have an umbrella?' asked Mick.

45

''Cause he hates the sun so much. Hats aren't good enough.'

'Why's he here if he hates the sun so much? Can't he go somewhere else?'

'Doesn't know anywhere else,' said Granpa. 'He's a Chinaman.'

'Where's Lamington?' asked Mick, suddenly worried about what might have happened to the cat.

'Under the bed. Doesn't like cyclones. When we've had enough we'll give him what's left of the fish. I've got VoVos and Anzac bickies for afters.'

Mick was disconcerted by the green bones, but the fish was delicious. Afterwards Granpa taught him how to play poker, having to shout the instructions, and then went and found the ludo and snakes-and-ladders board, left over from his son's childhood. Granpa took sips of Bundy, and let Mick have sniffs of it. They sang a few songs, and Mick asked what a waltzing matilda was, and Granpa said it was supposed to be a swag, but perhaps it was a woman called Matilda, and the swagman was telling her that she was going to come a-waltzing, ''cause what's the point of waltzing with a swag unless you were full as a goog and pretty damn desperate?'

'When we came here, we were squatters,' said Granpa. 'I'm a squatocrat. And now I've got a thoroughbred. Even if he's mad as a mother-in-law's cat. I've never given a swagman a hard time, though, and there's no trooper for miles.'

'I hope Willy's all right,' said Mick.

'We'll find out tomorrow,' said Granpa.

They became so used to the slamming and screaming of the cyclone that eventually they stopped paying attention to it, and fell asleep under the table. They were still asleep, propped against each other, when Lamington, finally certain that the cyclone was over, crept out from under the bed, jumped lightly on to the table, and polished their plates to a shine.

THE GIFT

When Mick came out in the morning, Granpa and the blackfellas were already clearing up the mess. 'G'day, Micko,' called Taylor Pete, and 'G'day' replied the boy.

It was a good day, too, with the sun shining brightly, and an unfamiliar humidity in the air. The paddock was a lake of water as far as the eye could see. It would have been beautiful, were it not for the wreckage of trees, the strewn planks, the gaps in the roofs of the sheds where the corrugated iron had been ripped off and hurled away, and the body of a Brahman cow wrapped up in the shattered timbers of the paddock fence. Jimmy Umbrella was re-erecting his outdoor cooking shack, one-handed, his umbrella firmly clutched in his left hand.

Mick went indoors and came back out with a brush.

He needed to be doing something useful like everyone else, and his bike needed cleaning up. It had rivulets of sand drying on it, and he knew that the air filter would be full of water. He could even see water under the glass of the speedometer, and when he removed the cover of the magneto, he found that that was full of water too. Taylor Pete came over, told him exactly what he had to do, and then left him to it. 'I'd lend a hand,' he said, 'but there's too much yakka on.'

Stemple came over and said exactly the same thing. It was the first really big cyclone he had ever been in, and he had genuinely questioned himself as to whether he had chosen a good place to live. He imagined that even being at war could not be more worrying than all that clattering, shrieking, howling and banging.

Granpa organised parties of men to go and find out what had happened to the mobs in the different paddocks. A lot of them would be bogged down, without a doubt. Granpa said they must have had a good eighteen inches of rain, and God knows what it must be like down near the creek. Mick wanted to go with them, but Granpa told him to get the bike working and then go out with a sack and try to find the chooks, otherwise there'd be no cackleberries till God knows when. 'And if you find Willy, let me know. I'll be out on the north paddock. He'll probably find his own way back, but I'm worried.'

It took two hours of dismantling, wiping, blowing and reassembling to get the old bike functioning again, but finally Mick put all his weight for a crisp thrust on the kick-start, and the engine came to life. He revved the engine for a while to make sure that it would not immediately pack up again, and went to fetch a sack from one of the sheds. It was then that he realised that the outdoor dunny had been blown away, apart from the pedestal, which sat there in solitary glory on its concrete plinth, its cracked porcelain glinting in the sunlight, with no sign of the wooden seat.

Mick soon found that there were not many places he could go where the bike would not sink in the new mud, and he realised that the best thing to do would be to head for the high ground so that he could have a good view. He returned and looked in the house for binoculars, but soon concluded that his grandfather must have taken them already.

He drove up the ridge that separated the farm from the creek, and was amazed to see that it had turned into an ocean. He felt like Cortez staring at the Pacific from a peak in Darien, and suddenly understood the wisdom of having constructed the homestead where it was, instead of closer to the water. He left the bike on the ridge, and scrambled down to the water's edge, walking along it in wonderment, having forgotten completely about the horse and the chooks. He thought there might be fish in it, and that it might be worth fetching a rod and reel.

He had gone half a mile along this new shoreline when he came to a stretch where there were a great

51

many leafless and unidentifiable shrubs half submerged. He looked out across the sheet of water, and became curious about one that seemed to have a lump in it. He shaded his eyes with his hands, and peered hard, but it was too painfully bright.

He thought he saw the lump move, and shook his head. He looked again, and was certain that it was moving. There must be an animal trapped out there.

Mick was a compassionate boy, and didn't like the thought of an animal dying out there, trapped in a shrub and getting steamed to death in the heat. On the other hand, he was intelligent enough to know that beneath the water there was a layer of new mud.

It was when he heard a whimpering sound that he decided to risk it.

Luckily he was near the edge, and it turned out that the mud was only six inches deep. Even so, it was scary enough, and with every cautious step he worried that he was going to die there. It was hard to extract one foot from the glutinous clinging mire, before putting down another. When he leaned forward to take the weight off his back foot, he could feel the remorseless suction that was trying to keep him immobile. His heart thumped in his chest, and the sweat prickled at his brow.

It turned out well. Mick carefully disentangled the puppy from the twigs that had enmeshed it. It was clearly very weak and exhausted, and was covered in thick blue slime. He had no idea what breed it might be, if it were any breed at all. He held it under the belly with one hand, and lowered it to the water so that he could give it a rinse and get the worst of the mud off, and then he tucked it under his arm and climbed back up the ridge to his bike. The puppy whined, but was too exhausted to struggle.

Mick put the dog in the sack, and drove home with it hanging from his right hand, so that he was unable to use the front brake properly. He stayed in low gear and made his way carefully.

When he arrived half an hour later, he carried the dog to the shower and cleaned it off thoroughly which was a difficult task, as the shower seemed to have only two settings, 'off' or 'ferocious'. It had no settings for subtle and gentle. In the end Mick took his clothes off and had a shower with the dog in his arms, as this seemed the only way out. Afterwards he rubbed it down with the sack, and sat on the veranda with the dog on his lap.

The puppy was male, and Mick judged that it was already weaned, because it accepted his gifts of small lumps of Lamington's rations, and then fell fast asleep.

That was how Granpa found them when he came home, and he didn't seem greatly surprised. 'That's a red cloud kelpie,' he said. 'What are you going to call it?'

'I don't know, Granpa.'

'You're not to call it Kevin.'

'No, Granpa.'

'Or Keith.'

'No, Granpa.'

Granpa took the dog from Mick's arms and held it up to look it in the eye. 'Bloody hell,' said Granpa. 'It's let one rip. Blimey. What a stinker.' He handed it back to his grandson. 'Here, you have it. If it's going to do that, it can be when someone else's holding it. And the dog's called "Blue". I always know what a dog wants to be called. It's hereditary. Gets passed down from your second uncle on your mother's side.'

'But he's red!'

'That's why he's called Blue. If you're short, you're called Lofty; if you're black, you're called Chalkie; if you're bald, you're called Curly; if you're fat, you're called Slim; if you're red, you're called Blue. Everybody knows that, son. By the way, we don't have dogs sleeping in the house. Our dogs are yard dogs. It's the rule, OK?'

'OK, Granpa.'

'What's the matter, son? You've got a face on you like half a mile of bad road.'

'Granpa, it's too cold out here at night. He's supposed to be snuggled up with his brothers and sisters, all in a heap.'

'It's the rule.'

'What if there's a dingo?'

'The other dogs'll see it off. Look, we'll find him a nice big box with a rug in it.'

That night Granpa looked in on Mick last thing, as he always did, to check that he was sleeping. It was the one time when he could just sit on the edge of the bed and look at his grandson's face, and stroke his hair, and think back to when his own small son slept in this very bed, and he would come in at night to check up on him. It was a world away, and Granpa could hardly believe that so much time had passed without his having noticed. He never let it show, but he was feeling more tired than he used to. Round here you had to stay young till the day you died, and there was nothing he was going to give up, not even entering the Roebourne Races on his one-eyed horse that had boomers loose in the top paddock, and always came in fourth or fifth in the wake of the blackfellas. He'd never won yet, but he wasn't going to stop trying now, aching hips or not.

On this night, Granpa frowned, and prised the puppy out of Mick's arms. There was a house rule, and it had to be stuck to. Only Lamington was allowed to sleep indoors at night, and the dogs stayed out. Granpa took the little dog outside and put it back in the box. The puppy wagged its tail so hard that it looked as though he was going to wag his backside off. Granpa looked into those small bright eyes, and said, 'Sorry, mate.'

The next morning he told Mick off, and said, 'My oath, you've got more front than bloody Myer's, you have. I told you that dogs sleep outdoors, and that's where they sleep, right? If you disobey me again, you'll be feeling the back of my hand. Understand?'

That night, Granpa came in to check up on Mick, and he wasn't there. There was no bedding either. Granpa went out onto the terrace, and found Mick curled up in his bedclothes with the puppy clutched to his chest. It was a very cold night. The two sleepers looked blissful.

Granpa prised the puppy out of his grasp, and restored it to its box. Then he picked up Mick and his bedding all in one armful, and carried him back to his bed without his even waking for a moment.

Granpa turned in, and had trouble sleeping. Amid the sound of the grasshoppers and nightbirds outdoors, he could hear the puppy whining. He thought about Mick. The boy had no friends of the same age. He had no mother or father to cuddle with. He had no brothers and sisters. In fact, the poor little sod didn't even have so much as a teddy bear. He was giving all his love to a motorbike.

Granpa knew exactly what it was like to be as alone as that. In the end he couldn't bear it any more, and he got up and went outside to fetch the dog. It yipped and squirmed in his arms, and tried to lick his face. Granpa put the dog back into Mick's arms, and wondered how he was going to announce the rule change in the morning. It would take some careful phrasing, so that it wouldn't look like a climbdown. He'd tell Mick that he'd thought about it, and decided that the nights were too cold after all, and he'd seen that perentie creeping about again.

In the morning, Mick said, 'Granpa, now that everything's wrecked, and everything's got to be mended, why don't we redo Granma's garden at the same time?'

'You know how to?'

'No. You can tell me what to do, and I'll do it.'

'We'll do it together,' said Granpa, 'but we'd better get everything else fixed first.'

BLIND WILLY

There were no longer many horses on the station because they had been replaced by motorcycles, and the few that remained were not much more than pets. None of them were particularly large, because the days when huge draught horses were needed to pull the carts had long gone. Nowadays you did not need to breed horses for a particular purpose, and so the general size had averaged out. Granpa delegated Taylor Pete to educate Mick.

First of all, Taylor Pete made Mick shut Blue away in the shed, and then showed him how to gain the confidence of a horse.

'Right, Micko,' he said, 'you come here and watch what I do.'

He walked softly up to Blind Willy and touched noses

with it. He sniffed the horse's breath, and the horse sniffed his. He patted the horse's neck, and the animal bared its teeth and took a friendly nip at the cloth of his shirt.

'Now you do it,' said Taylor Pete.

Mick let the horse sniff his breath, and then inhaled the breath of the horse. It smelled beautiful, like warm grass. It filled him with a kind of sensuous delight. The horse brushed his face with his lips, and they were very velvety and whiskery.

'Put your arms round his neck and lay your face against it,' said Taylor Pete, 'but nice and smoothly. No sudden moves.' Mick did as he was told, and after a while, Taylor Pete said, 'He likes you.'

'He's standing on my foot,' said Mick.

'Just you wait till he puts some weight on it,' said Taylor Pete. 'Now, if you always let a horse get to know you by exchanging breath, you can tame just about any old brumby pretty damn quick.'

'Is this all Aborigine stuff?' asked Mick.

'It's magic ancestral knowledge,' said Taylor Pete portentously, 'from the Dreamtime and beyond. It's all to do with smoke and dances and spells and magic bones, and then your ancestors plant the special knowledge in your brain without you having to learn it, and you wake up one morning full of horseness. I'll show you sometime.'

'Really?'

'No, just kidding. I worked it out for myself. If you

think about it, there weren't any horses here till the whitefellas brought 'em. Nothing to do with Dreamtime. Nightmare time, more like. It's like when you meet a cat; always let it sniff your fingers before you touch it. And I'll tell you something else. Did you know that horses are really a kind of rabbit?'

Mick shook his head.

'Well, rabbits and horses are both vegetarians and have peepers on the sides of their loaf, right? That means they can see behind them as well as in front, but they can't focus too well on anything very close. That's the main reason they can't read. Unless it's in big print quite a long way off. And rabbits and horses both kick with their back legs when they're in a blue.'

'Horses don't hop,' said Mick.

'Only 'cause they don't see the point,' replied Taylor Pete. 'And rabbits only hop 'cause they're jealous of boomers being so much bigger, and they want to be roos themselves, and they're hoping no one'll guess they're really rabbits.'

Every day for three months Mick went out to Blind Willy's paddock and exchanged breaths with him, because he had a plan. Gradually, Willy stopped kicking and rearing, and whinnying and caracoling, and peacefully took handfuls of lush grass from Granma's garden from Mick's outstretched palm. Then the day came when the horse let Mick lie across his back on his stomach.

Stemple had also become a keen rider, because he was relatively new to it, so he and Mick took to going out for a hack first thing in the morning and last thing in the evening, because it wasn't fair making horses work hard in the extreme heat of the day. Stemple's horse was small and tough, and Mick's was even smaller.

Stemple liked to talk about his plans. He was a guitar player, and one day he was going to study it properly, and become a truly good musician, even though at present he mainly played 'A Whiter Shade of Pale', and 'Where Have All the Flowers Gone', and 'Waltzing Matilda'.

Mick told Stemple that he wanted to be an armed policeman like his dad, and Stemple said it wasn't always easy having to fit into an organisation, the way that policemen and teachers had to. You were never your own man.

Blue always went with them, sniffing about, going off on tangents, often getting lost, but always arriving back home in the end. As far as Blue's nose was concerned, the station was an everlastingly interesting piece of paradise. There was nothing whatsoever whose whiff didn't tell a story. While Mick and Stemple talked about life, Blue had adventures alongside them that they could not possibly have imagined, in a world populated by wallabies, lizards, dingos and lady dogs.

Mick did not have enough money to buy presents, and in any case there wasn't a shop for miles, but at last there came a special day, and Mick had come up with something truly wondrous.

When Granpa was standing in the yard, Mick rode in with a grin on his face as wide as Cleaverville Beach. Granpa could not believe his eyes when he saw Mick on the thoroughbred. What he said is probably better left unrecorded, because it involved some ripe expletives, but he was undeniably amazed, thrilled and proud.

'Happy birthday, Granpa,' said Mick.

In the years to come, long after he had gone, Mick was usually remembered in that region as 'You know, the little boy who tamed that crazy half-blind horse'.

THE CAVE OF DREAMS

On his thirteenth birthday Mick's mother telephoned and said that she felt a little bit better, but not well enough to have him back yet. Mick said, 'Why don't you come and live here?' and she had replied, 'How's your dad? I haven't seen him in ages.'

Mick said, 'Dad's dead, Mum, you know he is. Granpa told me what happened.'

'Last time I saw him he was sleeping.'

'Oh, Mum …'

It was still no good trying to get through to her, and Mick's heart sank. He couldn't help but wonder if he would ever get his mother back.

Even so, Mick had a splendid birthday that turned out to be more interesting than he had expected. Mick was a few inches taller, his trousers were too short, his legs seemed terribly long for his body, and his voice had begun to crackle and break when he talked. He realised one day that he couldn't sing any more, and was starting to think about girls, even though he hardly ever saw one.

By now Blue had pretty much grown up, except that he was still full of puppy-dog energy and barminess. He was the colour of deep rust on a corrugated sheet. When he was dusty he seemed to melt into the landscape, but when he'd been for a swim in the creek he was a glossy dark russet. He had amber eyes, and ears so mobile that he almost seemed to be talking with them. He had quickly made friends with Lamington, which was fortunate for both of them, as Lamington did not like being chased, and Blue hated to have his nose raked.

Blue turned out to be very intelligent, energetic and bold, and he soon learned to ride on Mick's motorcycle, sitting between his legs with his paws on the tank, or even on the handlebars. It had been easy to learn because Mick had tucked him between his thighs on the seat when he was a tiny puppy, and the dog had simply grown up not knowing any different. It was not as dangerous as it might have been, because out on the station it was impossible to drive fast, and Granpa had given him some excellent advice: 'If you see an accident coming, never try to save the bike. You leap off and throw it away. If you try and save the bike, it'll rip you up and break your bones.'

Mick had quickly learned the wisdom of this, and he and Blue had only ever suffered bruises and grazes from their frequent spills. In fact, Blue sometimes saw the accidents coming before Mick did, and jumped off unbidden.

In the last year, Mick and his grandfather had remade Granma's garden, and now it was awash with zinnias and petunias, and sweet peas. They'd planted oleander, and set a bougainvillea up against the house. They had a bed of lettuce too, but it was rather too popular with the bugs, and they seldom had any left over for themselves. Almost every day Mick had to water the garden, sometimes two or three times, and he felt as though his arms were being stretched as long as an ape's because of having to carry the buckets. The best thing was that Granma's orange tree had recovered from the cyclone, and was bearing precious fruit that they could eat with special reverence, because there was so little of it.

Today, on his birthday, there was a disaster because in the mid-morning a plague of grasshoppers came along in a buzzing and clattering cloud, like something out of the Bible, and settled on every edible plant in the whole area. Mick could hardly believe it. There were millions and millions of them, and the sky went dark. He stood outside in wonder. Blue barked point-lessly, and Lamington skipped up and down on his hind legs, trying to bat them out of the sky. Eventually he caught one and went to the terrace to munch it, with its wings still buzzing at the sides of his mouth, like mad whiskers.

Granpa, Mick, Jimmy Umbrella and the blackfellas stationed themselves at the raised beds and tried to sweep the grasshoppers away from the flowers. About the rest of the farm they could do nothing, and their efforts to save the blooms were almost futile.

When at last the cloud of grasshoppers moved on, they left a ragged mess behind them, and thousands of dead and dying lying all over the ground.

Granpa looked at the wrecked garden and said resignedly, 'We'll have to start all over again.' He went indoors and came out with a cylindrical parcel, which he handed over to Mick. 'Sorry about the wrapping,' he said. 'Real men don't know how to wrap. Happy birthday, son.'

It was indeed wrapped extremely badly, in Christmas paper. It was wrinkled and ripped and asymmetrical, but it contained a beautiful torch, long enough to hold four big batteries. It was made of chromed steel, with a ring on the end that you could thread onto your belt. He turned it on, but it made no difference in the Pilbara sunlight. You simply couldn't tell, so he took it indoors and shut himself in a cupboard to make sure that it worked. He inspected the old rubbish that was stored there, and found a Slazenger tennis racket with broken strings, and a cricket ball.

When he came back out he said, 'Thank you, Granpa. It's the best torch.' He showed the cricket ball to Granpa and said, 'Can I play with this?'

68

'Don't see why not. And try not to run down the batteries when you don't need to, son. It's the one thing the store always runs out of.'

Granpa went to tell Taylor Pete something, and Mick fetched his motorcycle. He kicked it over to fire it up, and then when he was astride, Blue scrambled on, raking Mick's thighs with his claws, as usual. Off they went, weaving their way between the rocks and stunted trees, in the direction of the creek, with the new torch dangling from his belt. There were some caves that he had always wanted to explore. He was happy, even though his father had died and his mother was still not well. He had a motorbike, a torch, a dog and a magnificent grandfather, and over to his left there were three wallabies having a race with him over this hard and beautiful land.

The cave was in a low cliff by the creek, with a small entrance through which you had to crawl, and in the past Mick had found that the moment you crawled in, you blocked the light and could see nothing at all. It had always been very frustrating.

This time he went in on his hands and knees, wishing that he was wearing long trousers, and that his torch had been the kind that you could wear on your forehead. It was far too heavy to carry in his mouth too, and it was awkward trying to get in there with the torch in one hand when ideally you needed both hands on the ground.

The entrance passage was very short, and to Mick's

surprise it opened out into a small cavern, with a pool of bright clear water at the bottom. He flicked the torchlight around the walls and ceiling, and said, 'Wow.'

They were covered with Aboriginal etchings and paintings. Mick was not sure what a lot of them represented, but it seemed to him that he saw shapes like emus' feet, and spears, and lizards. There were patterns just like the ones you could see the blackfellas doing at Roebourne, and snakes. Blue came in and lapped at the water in the pool, and then sat and watched his master intently, as if on guard. Mick said, 'Hey, Blue, we could live in here, and be outlaws, and have orgies, like Ned Kelly.'

Mick did not know exactly what orgies were, or even that the Kellys had ever taken part in one, but he knew that outlaws had them, and they were very like rowdy parties. Blue grew restless and unhappy, and went back outside, and lay with his head between his paws, whining for Mick to come back out.

Mick shone the torch into the water and saw a beautiful piece of white quartz, shining and glittering. It was about a foot long, and two inches in diameter. Its ends were pointed, as if they had been bevelled. He tried to reach it, but it was too deep down, even if he lay flat. Just when he thought he was about to get it, with his right shoulder under the water, his torch went out. He felt a moment of extreme panic because of the intensity of the darkness, and he could feel his heart thumping in his chest. Sweat burst out at his temples and forehead, but then his eyes began to adjust, and he realised that there was light coming from the entrance. Even so, he had never felt more thoroughly spooked. He threw the torch out before him, and crawled into the daylight. He picked it up and tried to switch it on and off, but it had failed. The batteries could not have run down already, so the bulb must have burned out, thought Mick.

Back at the homestead, Mick found Taylor Pete tinkering with the fishplates on the wind pump. 'Happy birthday,' said Taylor Pete.

'How did you know?'

'Your grandad asked me to make you something.'

'What?'

'It's a secret.'

'Pete?'

'Yes?'

'Can you keep a secret?'

'I'm keeping one already. You got another one?'

'We found a cave, down at Myrie Pool.'

Taylor Pete suddenly looked very serious. 'You keep out of that, Micko, it's not for whitefellas, even half-growns.'

'You know it?'

'Of course I do. It's Yirramala. It's for Bunaga men. It's Dreamtime stuff.'

'What's Dreamtime?'

'It's stuff we dreamed up to fool the whitefella. It's all hokum.'

'Hokum?'

'Roo shit.'

'Really?'

'Just kidding. Did you see the white stone?'

'Yes, I couldn't reach it.'

'You shouldn't have tried. You never heard of Mukkine?'

'No.'

'He was a magic man, Micko. He bludgeoned a whitefella, and the troopers came after him, with another blackfella, because they reckoned you needed one to catch one, and that blackfella shot Mukkine. But you can't kill a Maban unless you get his thumb, 'cause that's where his power is. Understand?'

'Not really, Pete.'

'Doesn't matter. Anyway, Mukkine got in that cave and he put his spirit into that water, and that white stone is his stone, and if he points it at you, you die. And you'd better watch out because he might be after you already. Pass me that spanner … and that nut.'

Mick passed him the tool, and, in a very worried tone of voice, asked, 'Why would he come after me?'

'Land.'

'Land?'

'You people've got our land. This was ours. You took it. Fences went up. We couldn't wander. We got shot when we speared the sheep. We had to stay put and get work with the whitefella.'

'Granpa says we'll have to go one day.'

'The whitefellas? 'Spect so. Too late for us, though, Micko. We're like ghosts, still alive and haunting our own place.'

Mick looked sceptically at Taylor Pete, and thought that he did not remotely resemble a ghost. He asked, 'Do you speak Aborigine?'

Pete laughed. 'Aborigine? I'll tell you one thing. We had a whitefella here a while back. He was collecting languages, and he got me to talk a load of old baloney into a tape recorder. I made half of it up, the stuff I couldn't remember. I remembered a lot after he'd gone. There's no such thing as speaking Aborigine. I speak Yindjibarndi. There's blackfellas further north who mix it all up with English, and that's called Kriol, but I speak Yindjibarndi.'

'Can you speak me some?'

'Well, now, Roebourne is Yirramakartu, Whim Creek is Parrkapinya, and Cossack is Pajinhurrpa, and round here a boomerang isn't a boomerang. We call it something else, and there's fellas who can use it to knock birds out of the sky. You ought to go to Cossack. It's a graveyard.'

'A graveyard?'

'A graveyard of whitefellas' dreams. It's a ruin. And another thing; you're going to need protection. In case Mukkine comes after you. I'll do you a swap. Got anything nice?'

'I've got a dry bat and a tobacco tin,' offered Mick hopefully.

'I've got a roo's toe bone. I'll swap the bone for the tin.'

'Is it from that roo by the airstrip? I've already got the leg bones.'

'But you haven't got the toe bone I've got. Come on, swap.'

Taylor Pete dug into his pockets and produced a clasp knife, a piece of string, a paper clip and, finally, the toe bone. Mick took the bone, dug in his pocket and took out the tobacco tin.

'You punched holes in it,' said Pete.

'I've got a lizard inside,' said Mick.

'So you have,' said Pete, opening the tin.

'It's a rainbow skink.'

'Yeah. What did it do wrong?'

'Wrong?'

'Yeah, why's it in prison?'

'It's not.'

'Just a guest then?' Taylor Pete picked the tiny lizard out gently, and placed it in the shade of the wall. 'Now,' he said, 'you keep that bone on you at all times, and Mukkine won't come after you. And leave that white stone alone. That's blackfella business, got it? It stays where it is. The last whitefella who tried to get it fell in and drowned. In a few feet of water. Wasn't found for weeks.'

Mick nodded. 'Pete?'

'Yeah?'

'Did you go walkabout?'

'Course I did.'

'Isn't it hard? All that walking?'

'Don't be a galah. I went in the ute.'

That evening Jimmy Umbrella made a special birthday dinner of barramundi and mangrove oysters, with peas from a tin, and something black and crispy as a side dish. Just as Granpa and Mick were about to tuck in, the generator failed. 'Damn it,' said Granpa, as the lights went out. 'You got that torch I gave you? I'm going to have to find some lamps.'

'It's on my belt,' said Mick, 'but I think the bulb's gone.'

'What? Already? Hand it over, will you?'

Mick undid the buckle of his belt and passed the torch over in the dark. Granpa slid the switch, and shone the beam vertically from under his chin, so that he looked like a sinister ghost. 'Nothing wrong with that,' he said, and a shiver ran down Mick's spine. This was all somewhat spooky. Why would it only work when it wasn't in the cave?

Granpa fetched some paraffin lamps and lit them, and then went to find his bottle of Bundy. 'Have a sniff,' he said, 'and many happy returns. Here's to your mum getting back on the straight and narrow.'

They ate happily in the semi-darkness, the lamps filling the room with a pleasantly faint aroma of paraffin.

Granpa said, 'I saw you talking with Taylor Pete, a good long time. He's the only one of our blackfellas who ever says much. Most of them don't. They can work side by side for hours and not say a damn thing. They don't do small talk. And they don't like questions.'

'Pete doesn't mind,' said Mick.

'You know he'll tell you any old rubbish, just for fun?'

Mick held up one of the blackened crispy objects impaled on his fork. 'Granpa, what are these? They're really bonzer.'

'Grasshoppers, son. They call it entomophagy. No point in wasting 'em. Got the idea off the cat. Blue had a go at 'em too.'

TRAINING BLUE

Five mornings later, Mick found out what Taylor Pete had been making for him. It was a cricket bat, crude and heavy, but nicely balanced, and just the right length. Pete had laminated three thick planks, and then trimmed it all down, varnished it, and wound the handle with rubber from an old inner tyre, to take some of the shock and sting out of hitting the ball. Then he had painted three stumps in white paint on the wall of the shed.

'It's a dinkum bat, Peeto,' said Mick, his eyes shining with pleasure.

'Don't thank me, thank your grandad,' said Taylor Pete. 'It's actually a present to himself.'

'A present to himself?'

'He's had no one to play cricket with since your dad left. That bat's for him, so he can play with you.'

77

'But it's too small.'

'I'll probably have to make him another. I think we've got a word for that. In Yindjibarndi.'

'For a cricket bat?'

'Nah. In Yindjibarndi, a cricket bat is a "cricket bat". I mean, "a present for yourself". Can't remember what it is, though. It'll come back later, when I'm at something else.'

Granpa made Mick play cricket almost every morning, until the sun grew too hot, and the light so bright that it was senseless trying to follow a ball. Stemple usually passed by on purpose in order to be invited to join in. He was a fine wicketkeeper, but as the stumps were painted on a wall, he had to make do with being cover point. He could bowl a mean googly even on that dust, and often had arguments with Granpa about LBW. Granpa reckoned there was no chance that Stemple had got him out, and Stemple reckoned he got him every time, but as there was no umpire, Stemple's appeals were formally undecidable, no matter how much he ran in circles pumping the air with his fist and shouting, 'Howzat?'

Mick had to admit that his grandfather was a very good cricketer. He could dive to catch a ball, and roll over like a paratrooper as he struck the ground, coming up covered in red dust, but unhurt. He could hurl the ball from just about any distance, and land it square on the stumps. He could break windows with a cut, and could pull off an ugly cow shot that sent the ball high into the sky and into Willy's paddock. Once he scored sixty-three runs while Mick went looking for the ball, and then declared, as he was too tired to bat on. He could drive the ball along the ground straight back at Mick, so that he had to leap out of the way, and he could bowl a spinner that seemed to bounce sideways at forty-five degrees in either direction, so that Mick didn't stand a chance at the crease unless he bounded forward and took the balls at full toss. Sometimes he would bowl a ball so hard and fast that the side of the shed was at risk of being wrecked and so Taylor Pete nailed up a thick piece of ply to protect it.

After one of their games, Mick said, 'This is just like having Dad back,' and Granpa had looked away and said, 'Yeah, it is. It's very like.'

One day Mick went into Willy's paddock to collect the ball while his grandad ran twenty-six runs, and found the horse going bonkers. What he did not know was that the ball had landed in between the horse's forelegs when he had been grazing, and startled him so greatly that he had reared up and screamed. He was still rearing and screaming, and kicking up his hind hooves, when Mick arrived to find the ball. He managed to retrieve it, but was promptly chased out of the paddock by the horse, which was clearly trying to take a bite out of his backside. Mick did not have a chance to close the gate, and that is how Willy escaped, pursuing the poor boy round the corner and into the yard, and that was how Granpa and Mick found themselves up the ladder to the water tank. Blue found himself running round it in circles, and Lamington found himself on the roof of the shed. They were up there for half an hour before Willy calmed down and settled into chewing what was left of Granma's garden. Granpa said, 'I keep telling you always to close the gate of Willy's paddock. I've got a good mind to dock your pocket money.'

'It was me who tamed him,' said Mick, from above him. 'And you don't give me pocket money.'

'I give you something when you need it,' said Granpa.

'Anyway, Willy's almost all right these days,' said Mick. 'It doesn't matter too much if he gets out.'

'Yeah, we've had much madder horses than that, mad as a meat axe,' said Granpa. 'I wish you'd been here when we had horses instead of motorbikes. The black-fellas were the best jackaroos. Those were the days. Taylor Pete wasn't half bad on a horse when he was a kid. He won at Roebourne every time. They had to shut the tote when he was on.'

In all their cricket games, Blue had played his part. He was entirely obsessed with having the ball, so woe betide you if you dropped a catch. If the ball was struck a great distance, there was no chance of keeping up with Blue as he hurtled after it, and then it was a hopeless job trying to get it off him. It didn't matter how much you tried to prise his jaws open. It didn't work even if you pinched his nose to stop his breathing. You could shout 'Drop!' or 'Give!' and Blue would just pull back, wag his tail, and make strange grunting noises that were like half a growl. The worst thing was that if you finally got the ball off him, it was covered with the most slimy slobber imaginable, and would have to be rolled in the dust under your foot to get it all off.

'It's time you trained that dog,' said Granpa one day. 'An untrained red cloud is a damned liability. That dog can't even sit.'

'But how do you train dogs, Granpa?'

'Never had to,' Granpa replied, shrugging his shoulders. 'The blackfellas always trained our heelers.'

At first Mick tried teaching by example. He sat up and begged, he presented his paw, he lay down, he rolled over, and even tried to sit like a dog. Nothing worked, and Blue just observed him with puzzled curiosity, as did anyone else who witnessed it. It looked as though Blue was training Mick, because he would bark, and the boy would lie down.

One day Taylor Pete came across Mick trying to teach Blue. Mick was repeating 'Sit! Sit!' in a commanding tone of voice, and pressing down on Blue's hindquarters. Blue was giving way a little, and immediately springing back up again. That dog was surprisingly strong.

'You've got no idea, have you, Micko?' said Pete.

'I've tried and tried and tried,' said Mick, 'but I've got nowhere.'

'Food,' said Pete. 'They'll do anything for food. It's the only thing you need to know. I'll bring you some scraps tomorrow.'

In the morning Taylor Pete gave Mick a bag of small dark cubes. 'What are these?' asked Mick.

'Dried roo. Diced.' Pete popped one into his mouth, and said, 'You should try some. They're nice. You can suck 'em for hours. Not that Blue will.'

Mick did try one, reluctantly, because he did not want to seem a sissy in front of Taylor Pete. It was rock hard, but it had a rich dark taste, and so Mick left it in the corner of his mouth to soften up, and it did last for hours.

They did not last with Blue. They were gulped straight down, and Mick got through an awful lot of diced dried roo meat before he was done with training that dog, but by the end of it Blue could even jump through the window of a ute on command, and get halfway up a gum tree before falling off. The only thing that Blue could not be trained out of was letting rip with stinkers, and the dried meat only made that worse. He got used to being sent out when he was windy, and would sit outside the door whining to be let back in, and raking at it with his forepaw. It would be fair to say that his prowess in the stench department was fast becoming a local legend.

Mick was happy, and the sadness of his father's death and his mother's absence was something that mainly afflicted him late at night, if he woke up and had trouble returning to sleep.

Granpa had very big worries, however, and he was trying not to let them show. It was not that Blue had now become an excellent retriever, and it was no longer possible to pull off thirty runs while Mick looked for the ball in Willy's paddock.

Granpa was anxious because there was a persistent rumour that the iron company wanted to put a railway track through the station. What worried Granpa even more was that a few weeks ago Mick's mother had discharged herself from hospital and disappeared somewhere in Sydney. He did not have the heart to tell the boy.

EDUCATION

Granpa told Mick that from now on he was going to have a tutor to make sure he did all the work for his correspondence courses. Granpa was concerned that the boy's education had become very random and patchy indeed. He had neither the time nor the inclination to teach the boy himself, and was beginning to feel that he was letting him down. He couldn't expect Mick to make a future for himself with nothing but a headful of his grandfather's anecdotes.

'Your new tutor is seventy years old, and she looks like a goanna, and she whacks you with a belt if you're a slacker,' said Granpa. 'She's only got one tooth, in the middle of her mouth, and she's got lizard breath, and she hasn't washed her armpits or changed her knickers for forty years. That's the only kind of teacher to have.

85

She's called Mrs Marble, 'cause that's how hard her heart is. And it doesn't pump blood, it pumps bladder juice.'

Accordingly, on the day that she was due to arrive, Mick and Blue went to Cossack on the Francis-Barnett, just to put off the evil hour when he would have to meet her. It was a blistering hot morning, and Mick had his dad's wide-brimmed hat pulled down over his eyes, and a large handkerchief tied around his lower face so that he would not have to breathe in all the dust. He looked very like a bandit from an old cowboy film.

Cossack was a sad ruin, not least because people had been pillaging the old buildings for timbers that they could use in their own. Many of these timbers had originally come from ships, and had naval markings on them, as you often found in the timbers of cottages in the Old Country. In Mick's time, there were a few little Aboriginal boys fishing off the old harbour wall; a selection of dead people in the old cemetery outside of town, many with exotic names; one family of Greek fishermen who were always out at sea; and one person living in a ruin.

Mick met Sergeant Sam the first time he went to Cossack, finding him relaxed in a deckchair on the veranda of a derelict house, with a rough roof over him that had been knotted together out of vegetation and strips of plank.

Sergeant Sam was an old soldier, a tall thin whitefella

with a large hooked nose, whose clothes were pretty filthy, and who wore shoes whose soles flapped as he walked. He had come back from the war in Vietnam, and decided that he truly did not want to live among humans any more. He had a long white scar on his back, and burns on his legs.

Sam had said, 'G'day, mate,' to the boy and the dog, and Mick had replied, 'G'day.'

'What do you want?'

'I came to look around,' said Mick. 'Granpa said it was interesting.'

'It used to be interesting. Now it's a big barrel of bugger all, worse than Bunbury. That's why I like it.'

'Do you … do you live here?' asked Mick.

'Yup.'

'Oh.'

'Aren't you going to ask me why?'

'If you like.'

'I don't like or not like. Don't you want to know?'

'Yes, please.'

'It's because I'm a bloody hermit. That's a nice mutt you've got there. Red cloud kelpie. That's what I always had.'

'This is Blue,' said Mick.

'Hello, Blue,' said Sam, holding out his hand, and Blue raised his paw for a shake. 'Bonzer polite dog,' said Sam.

'I taught him that,' said Mick.

'Well, you're a fine boy then, aren't you, mate?'

Mick came back to see Sergeant Sam regularly, bringing him things he might need, such as toothpaste and string, and paraffin for his Primus stove. The little Aborigine boys sometimes gave him a fish, and all in all the Cossack hermit led a nice simple life with no worries except running out of water, and he wasn't such a hermit after all, because of the occasional presence of the Greek fishermen living there too, in the old Courthouse. Before that there had been another hermit, but he had left when Sam had arrived, on the grounds that the place was getting too crowded.

Sergeant Sam told Mick all about how the town had risen and fallen, beginning with a ship called the *Mystery*, which, in 1863, had failed to find a landing place at Port Hedland or De Grey. On its sister ship, the *Tien Tsin*, there had been a cargo of cattle in desperate need of water and fodder. Here in Cossack they had found the Harding River nearby, and plenty of places where wells yielded water, and so that was how Cossack accidentally came to be.

Sergeant Sam showed Mick where the horse-drawn tram used to run, and the railway to Roebourne, whose cars were pulled by teams of oxen. He showed him where the huge fleet of pearling luggers used to anchor in the cyclone season, and he took him to wasteland near the cemetery, which used to be a town of hundreds of Japanese pearlers, and Malays, and Afghans, and Chinese, complete with gambling joints, opium dens, stabbing and brawling, and rowdy houses of ill repute.

'Just imagine it,' said Sam, 'and look at it now. There was a riot when a boatload of Jap women turned up, once. Now it's just dry grass and baked earth, and not a Jap woman for miles.'

'Granpa always says that everything passes away, and something else comes in its place,' Mick told him.

'Your granpa's right,' replied Sam, 'but the only thing that came instead was me.'

Sam told Mick about Emma Withnell, the first woman to arrive, who raised eleven children, and then there was Caroline Platt, who was always in trouble with the law for getting into fights, wrecking things, and even beating up the schoolmistress. And then there was Susan Thompson. 'A true blue scarlet woman,' said Sam, and Mick wondered what on earth he meant.

Then there came the Gold Rush, and then leprosy arrived, which infected the blackfellas, and they had to build a lazaret for the poor victims on the other side of the river, and all that was left of it now was a few lumps of concrete.

Sam showed Mick the remains of the turtle-soup factory, and the Aboriginal petroglyphs down at Settler's Bay, whose age nobody knew. 'Everything grows up, and then passes away,' said Sam. 'Take my advice, son. Think of every day as a new bash at life.'

'Is that what you do?'

Sam looked confounded and abashed, and replied, 'Too late for me, mate. And don't do as I do, do as I say.'

All in all, Sergeant Sam was as friendly a hermit as

one could ask for, and a boy and a dog could waste a whole day very happily in his company. Quite inadvertently, Mick learned a great deal from him about how to winkle the history out of archaeological remains.

Another important influence was Mrs Marble.

When Blue and Mick got home just before dark, covered in the usual and universal red dust, they found that Granpa had been pulling a fast one. Mrs Marble was really Miss Marble. She could not have been a day over twenty, and every man on the station had already fallen in love with her, apart from Granpa, who had learned to value the peace and quiet that comes from being unattached. In the days to come he was to enjoy the spectacle of all the station hands turning up, hiding behind corners, or idling nearby while attempting to look busy. One day Taylor Pete even cut himself on purpose, so that Miss Marble could tend to the wound.

Miss Marble had curly blonde hair, an upturned nose and eyes of periwinkle blue. Her voice had a laugh in it, and she smelled pleasantly of lavender. 'Call me Betty,' she said to Mick, but Mick was so entranced that he couldn't call her anything at all. His mouth flapped up and down like a spare sock on a washing line.

Unfortunately Miss Marble had arrived on the same plane as the bush doctor, and Mick had to endure the pain and humiliation of receiving a vaccination in the backside, even though he had begged to have it in the arm. Betty Marble left the room when Mick was told to take down his trousers, and for this Mick remained grateful for the rest of his life.

That night Betty lay in her room, her mind awhirl with her new adventure, and prevented from sleeping in any case by the racket of all the nocturnal creatures outside. In the room next door, Mick lay awake, thinking how strange and wonderful it was to have a woman sleeping in the room next door. His mother seemed a distant dream to him now, something beautiful that shimmered in the imagination, but could not be touched.

In his room, Granpa lay awake, worrying, because the bush doctor had examined him, and had not been entirely happy with the state of his heart. Granpa had become so used to being indestructible that he could hardly manage to think of himself as anything else. That night he decided that he was not going to be careful. He was the kind of man who would always go at it full tilt, regardless. If he was going to go, it would be from lifting a ute out of a ditch, or falling off Blind Willy at Roebourne Races.

In his quarters, Stemple also lay sleepless. From the moment that he had set eyes on Betty at the landing strip, he had fallen head over heels.

OF UNDERWEAR,
EDUCATION AND MUSIC

Two days after Betty's arrival, there came Mick's first proper school day, and he had made himself very smart, even slicking his hair into place with water. He had spent a quarter of an hour sorting his pencils, rubbers and exercise books into neat and workmanlike order on the table. Clearly he was already in love with Betty, as was everyone else except for Granpa and Blue. The dog had already worked out that she was a bad influence.

While he waited, he looked out over the yard, trans-fixed, because he had never before seen a young woman's underwear hanging on a clothes line. It was a strange feeling, knowing where those clothes had been. And there was something unbelievably feminine about them. Not far down the line were his own underpants, which used to be white, but were now a dull shade of cream, with a big ragged hole through the seat. Next to them was Granpa's baggy, ripped, oil-stained contribution to the underwear collection. He felt ashamed to see them in such proximity to Betty's pristine lacy delicates.

Then Blue turned up in the yard, and he noticed the new items hanging from the line. Before Mick knew it, he was watching Blue leaping up and down, as if he were a living canine pogo stick, trying to grab a brassiere, and by the time that he had run out into the yard, Blue had already got himself triumphantly entangled in its elasticated straps, and was moving in circles, wondering what to do with himself.

Mick fetched Betty, and fortunately she was a good sport and saw the funny side of it, and ran indoors to get her Kodak. Then Mick untangled Blue, and Betty walked off with her brassiere to wash it all over again while Taylor Pete raised the height of the line. That first day, lessons began late.

Mick was sitting by the radio set, adjusting the tuning, when Betty walked in with books under her arm. What Mick did not know or suspect was that she had been quite nervous about her first day as a teacher, and had got up early to plan what she was going to do. Now she exuded an air of absolute confidence and professionalism that belied what she truly felt inside, which was a combination of embarrassment about the underwear incident and the nervousness of a novice.

Betty and Mick sat by the radio set and put on their headphones. There was a crackling noise, and then a voice came through, saying, 'Now have we got Tom and Sally from Summerhill and Mick and Betty from Karratha? Good. How's it going? Today we're doing geometry, or more correctly, trigonometry, and we're going to start with the equilateral triangle. Incidentally, boys and girls, my dad was an engineer, and he used to say, "If you want something strong, make it out of triangles," so listen in, all you budding engineers, this might be useful …'

Mick and Betty sat side by side happily doing what the School of the Air told them to do. Not half an hour had gone by when Betty suddenly stood up, pinching her nostrils together and flapping her left hand in the air, exclaiming, 'Mick! That's horrible! Go out and get to the dunny straight away.'

'It wasn't me, Miss.'

'Well, it certainly wasn't me! Does that smell like a lady's?'

'Does it smell like a boy's, Miss?'

'Well, I wouldn't be surprised. You know what boys are made of.'

'Well, it isn't, Miss. Don't worry, Miss, you get used to it.'

'Used to it? Not in a month of Sundays! Go on, get out and get rid of it, and don't come back till you have!'

'It wasn't me, Miss. It was Blue. He's under the table.'

Betty bent down and looked into Blue's amber eyes. The dog thumped his tail on the floor, but it did him no good.

'Out!' she cried.

'But, Miss, it's his house too. He can't help it if he's got rank guts, Miss.'

Betty put her hands on her hips and said, 'It's either him or me.'

Blue wandered out into the heat with a strong sense of grievance in his heart. He personally had no objection to his spectacular pongs, and did not see why anyone else should. Surely it was a matter for congratulation? Somewhat bitterly and dejectedly he set off up the track out of the homestead, because his nose told him that there was a bitch somewhere in the middle distance who might be inclined to be friendly. He began to feel happier, and settled into a comfortable trot. How wonderful it was to be a dog in the wilderness, with no worries because of all the tame humans. No worries except for the female ones, anyway. There was some taming to do there, that was for sure.

Towards the end of daylight, ten miles out, when he was driving back from Roebourne, Granpa saw something come out into the middle of the road ahead of him, about a quarter of a mile off. He couldn't make it out because of the shimmering heat haze and at first he thought it must be a crazy dingo. As he drew near, he realised it was Blue, and stopped the ute. The alternative would have been to run him straight over.

'Blimey, mate, you're a long way out,' he said. 'And you're a walking dust heap. Hop in.'

Blue leapt into the back of the ute and settled down. Granpa drove carefully home, because more than once he had lost a dog from the back by swinging round corners too fast. In fact the vet in Roebourne had told him it was the most common cause of dog injuries in these parts, but at least it wasn't as bad as the dogs that came in poisoned by dingo bait. The vet reserved his best expletives and most white-hot anger for the drongos who put out dingo bait.

That evening they all had dinner outside because it wasn't too hot, all the men together at the great long rough old table. Granpa set out hurricane lamps, and put a couple of bulbs on an extension lead. He said it was a special welcoming dinner for Miss Betty, and there was to be no swearing, no belching, no chundering, no letting rip with trumpeting trouser busters, no filthy jokes and no fighting.

'What's the point, then?' asked Taylor Pete, but he turned up anyway, because Jimmy Umbrella was going to do a proper barbie for once, instead of all the interesting

97

things that Granpa normally liked to eat. A slab of steak and some snaggers was right up Taylor Pete's street. He arrived just as Jimmy was firing up the barbecue and reminded him that he liked his steak still mooing.

Stemple was extra smart that evening. He had even thought of putting on a tie, but that was going too far for a proper westsider to contemplate, and in any case, having spent some time turning out his drawers, he realised that he didn't have one. He arrived with clean clothes and polished shoes, and his guitar on the passenger seat of his ute.

Stemple was the best local musician, and that was because there was no competition. He would get two verses into a song and then forget the words. He would start the song again, and forget the words in exactly the same place. This could go on for a long time. Sometimes he would remember the words but not the chords, and would stop and fiddle around on the guitar as he tried to find the right one. That was difficult, because how do you find the right chord when you are not singing in tune anyway? Luckily, by the time that Stemple got around to playing at parties, the men were already four sheets to the wind, and beyond caring.

Thanks to Granpa's prohibitions, it was extremely awkward for anyone to think of anything to say, and at first the evening turned out to be somewhat sticky. The men ate quietly, sneaking sideways glances at the lovely Miss Betty Marble, and when they wanted to let rip they left the table and sneaked behind the shed. Only

Blue did any different. He ate a pack of raw snaggers, and the gristly lumps off the steaks that the men flicked over to him, and made the night intermittently aromatic, as was his wont.

It was such an awkward evening that all they managed to talk about was ping-pong. The men played a lot of ping-pong when they were not swimming, shooting, fishing, or out on the lash in Roebourne.

'I'll teach you, if you like,' said Stemple to Betty, and she replied, 'No need. I'm already damned good.'

The men were a little taken aback. Did she say 'damned'? Did real ladies say 'damned'? Did that mean that they could say it too?

'I'll give you a game,' said Stemple.

'You're on,' said Betty. 'I'll bet you a kiss.'

'A kiss?' repeated Stemple, dumbfounded.

'Yeah, if you win, I kiss Mick on the top of the head, and if I win, you kiss the dog.'

'Blimey,' was all that Stemple could say. This was a lairy lady indeed.

'Stemple plays the guitar,' said Mick suddenly.

Stemple shot him a mean glance, because at heart he knew he was a rotten musician, and didn't want to have to show himself up. He'd brought his guitar out of vanity, half hoping that no one would ask him to sing.

'Oh, what do you play?' asked Betty.

'Um, not much. Rock and roll, a bit of Dylan, a bit of Tom Paxton.'

'Do you play "A Whiter Shade of Pale"? I just love that. Can't get it out of my head sometimes.'

Mick said, 'He plays that a lot, but …' He was going to say 'but it's really terrible', but stopped himself just in time.

'It's bloody terrible,' said Taylor Pete. 'You don't want to wrap your ears round that.'

'Bloody cheek,' retorted Stemple.

'It's true, though,' said Taylor Pete.

'You want to watch it, mate,' said Stemple, his colour rising.

'No blues, boys,' said Granpa. 'Remember what I said.'

The long and short of it was that, out of sheer manly pride, Stemple had to fetch his guitar from the ute, tune it up as approximately as he could, and have a go at 'A Whiter Shade of Pale'. His hands were sweaty, shaky and slippery, and perspiration ran from his temples. He had never felt more in need of a saviour. He offered a silent prayer to the god of desperate musicians, whoever that was. There wasn't anything in the world more important on that day than making a good impression on Betty Marble.

He began to sing that famous first line, but immediately there came a howl from under the table. Blue liked making music, and this was the first time he had had any accompaniment, apart from when he sang along to the whistle of the kettle. He was going to make the most of it. 'Owwwwwwwwww, owwwwwwwwwww,' he sang. In the near distance, the dingos joined in.

Everybody laughed, and Stemple, who couldn't believe his luck, said, 'Sorry, Miss, I can't compete with that.'

'Never mind, Stemple, you did your best. Can I see the guitar?'

Stemple handed it over, and Betty adjusted the tuning. She began to pluck it delicately, and then sang softly. As she grew bolder she let her voice ring out. She sang 'Silver Dagger', 'Ten Thousand Miles', 'Black Is the Colour', 'Boots of Spanish Leather', 'The Last Thing on My Mind'. She had a sweet clear soprano voice, a little breathy, but with perfect articulation. Blue and the dingos fell silent, as did the many animals of the night. The men put their hands in their laps and just listened. This was the most beautiful evening of their lives. What can you do when something so sublime happens so unexpectedly? These songs made them think of what they had lost, and of what they hoped to win. This pretty young woman seemed to be singing of what was so well hidden in their hearts that they had never been aware of it before. She made Mick think of his father in his grave, and his mother mad with grief. Granpa thought about Granma, and his son, and the years left to him if he was lucky.

When Betty had had enough, she quietly propped the guitar against the table, and said, 'Sorry for going on so long. I get carried away.'

The men were so moved that they hardly knew how to react. Clapping and cheering just would not have been reverent enough. Granpa got to his feet with a tot of Bundy in his hand, but found it difficult to speak. Eventually he managed to say, 'I've never heard anything so damned good in all my life. Welcome to the homestead, Betty. Let's have music every day.'

The men got to their feet and toasted a welcome, straight out of their tinnies.

After the party was over and everyone had left, apart from Betty and Stemple, she asked him, 'Do you think I could borrow your guitar sometimes? I feel kind of lost without one. I've been kicking myself for leaving mine behind, but everyone said it would come unglued in the heat.'

'You can have it, Miss.'

'No, I couldn't. How about a day on and a day off?'

'Why aren't you, you know, doing that for a living, Miss?'

'I will be,' said Betty confidently. 'I'm going to go to Paris. After this. Did you know there's just been something called "The Summer of Love"?'

'No, Miss.'

'Well, there has been. Doesn't that sound wonderful?'

'It does, Miss.'

'I don't want to miss any more summers of love. I'm going to Paris and I'm going to busk on the banks of the Seine, and I'll go to London, and maybe San Francisco.'

'You're in the right place,' said Stemple. 'Out here in the Pilbara, everyone passing through is a dreamer.

This is the land where dreams are hatched. Then you go away and make them true. And all your life you dream of the Pilbara, where your dreams were made, because this place gets to you. But you never come back. That's what they say.'

'Stemple?'

'Yes, Miss?'

'You know that bet about the dog?'

'Yes, Miss.'

'Well, it's all right. You wouldn't have had to kiss the dog.'

He thought of what she might mean, and asked, 'I get to kiss Mick on the top of the head, right?'

She put her arms round his neck and shook her head in the darkness. Her eyes seemed dark and liquid. 'Not what I meant at all,' she whispered.

'Do I have to beat you at ping-pong?'

'No. Not really. You don't have a dog's chance of doing that.'

And that was how their first kiss came about, behind the pump house, with a big moon lofted like a Chinese lantern in the sky, and Stemple's guitar hanging on its strap upside down on his back, and the tune of 'Amazing Grace' still going round and round in his head.

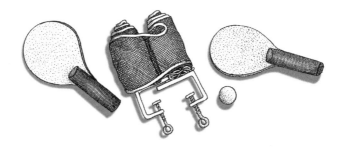

DISGRACE

Stemple had to swallow a great deal of pride in order to be with a girl as gifted as Betty, and it wasn't just that she thrashed him at ping-pong every time, 21–0, even when she played left-handed. It was the way that she thrashed him. She could do serves with different kinds of spins on them, and you never knew what they were going to be until it was too late. She could do a forehand smash with so much top spin that it didn't even bounce, it just landed and rolled. She could do a backhand that put the ball on the edge of the white line every time. Everybody was amazed by it. Stemple asked her how she had got to be so good, and she said it was all because of her dad. He used to put a coin on the table, and let her keep it if she could land a ball on top of it, and that was how she had saved up enough for a ukulele, which was what she had played before she graduated to her first guitar.

The one thing that Stemple loved more than anything else was playing on the guitar and singing to it, but, compared to Betty, he had been forced to realise that he was just another happy basher and hopeless cater-wauler. He wanted to be better than that.

He came round almost every evening to be humiliated at ping-pong and take a music lesson. He had had no idea just how much there was to learn. Betty played scales and made him sing them back to her. As the days went by he found he could sing both higher and lower than he used to. She showed him chords that looked impossible to play, and many of them really were impossible when you first tried them. She showed him how to pick the strings instead of just strumming, and how to make the beat rock, with your right thumb bouncing between the bass strings. She made him play beyond the first position, until he knew the names of every note on every fret of every string, and knew the shapes of all the movable chords. She showed him how to damp the bass strings with the heel of his hand so that they thudded instead of ringing out, and she showed him how to do the calypso slap so that he could play 'Island in the Sun' and 'Jamaica Farewell'.

Stemple endured the mockery of his friends, who had lost a boozing partner, and put up with them taunting him with 'You're a girl's man now, mate. You're beyond help, you are.' Stemple would reply, 'Jealousy will get you nowhere, mate.'

His mates were jealous, of course. It was impossible not to be, but at the same time they could see that Betty and Stemple were happy together and had a common bond. He had arrived in the Pilbara wanting to be a jackaroo, to lead the wild outdoor Australian life, only to find that horses were going out of use on the stations. In any case, being a jackaroo was only something he had wanted to do before going on to higher things, except that he did not yet know what these higher things were.

Betty was also going on to higher things, but she knew exactly what they were. It seemed to them both that they would be going off and doing them together. Stemple took a few days off and cadged a lift on a road train to Perth, returning with another guitar, several sets of strings and a fiddle, because Betty knew how to play that too. He had managed to find a guitar whose glue wouldn't melt in the Pilbara heat, but the fiddle didn't last long, and Taylor Pete had to put it back together for Betty, even though he had never worked on an instrument in his life. He made his own little clamps, with four-inch bolts, and slices of dowel. The odd thing about that trip was that Blue had wanted to come along too, so Stemple let him. Naturally, they had often had to open the windows of the cab.

Stemple and Betty sat face-to-face on the veranda trying out duets together. They began to compose their own songs. She said she wanted to be like Judith Durham from the Seekers. They talked about Paris and San

Francisco, and about folk songs and protest songs, and whether the Beatles or the Rolling Stones were better. They held hands in the dark, and lingered a terribly long time when kissing farewell at night.

The only one who was not happy for them was Mick. He was new to love, and the feelings were welling up in him in a manner that was frightening. It was like having a raging beast inside, where before there had only ever been a tame pup.

Mick was profoundly in love with his teacher. He did everything he could to please her, and did wonderful work in his exercise books. When she put her hand lightly on his shoulder and leaned over to look at something he had done, he loved the tickle of her hair against his face, and the sweet scent of her breath.

Mick began to hate Stemple, even though they had always been good mates, and they had learned to ride together. He hated Stemple for taking Blue to Perth without asking, and he hated him for taking Betty away from him. He had the same stupid thought going through his mind all the time, on a loop that just wouldn't stop turning. He was thinking, 'Stemple's six years older than her, and I'm six years younger, so what's the problem? Six years is only six years, is only six years, is only six years …'

One day Mick couldn't stand the jealousy any more, and knew that something had to be done about it. He left his lesson when Betty was briefly out of the room, and, his pencil still in his hand, walked out into the heat of the midday to find Stemple. He was cleaning out Willy's water trough, with Lamington in attendance and the mad horse not far off, kicking at the fencing. Mick faced Stemple, trembling with just enough rage to overcome his fear.

'What's up, mate?' asked Stemple.

Mick raised his fists. 'You put 'em up!' he said.

'What?' said Stemple, his eyebrows practically going over the back of his head.

'Put 'em up!' repeated Mick. 'Come on!'

'Bugger off,' said Stemple, but in a friendly manner.

'Coward!' said Mick.

'What's all this about?'

'You know what it's about!'

'I surely don't, mate.'

'You keep away from her. She's mine, not yours!'

'Oh cripes,' said Stemple, cottoning on at last. 'Look,' he said, 'I didn't know you felt that way. But you should've asked her first before you tried to pull one like this, shouldn't you, mate? A girl isn't yours just because you say she is. She's got to be of the same opinion, right? And I don't fight little boys.'

'I'm not a little boy!'

'No, no, you're right, mate, you're a kind of in-betweener. But I'm still not fighting. Understand? Now get back to your schoolroom, and we'll just forget all about this, right?'

Mick came at Stemple with his fists flailing, and caught him a few blows on the chest. Stemple grabbed his wrists, and Mick took to kicking him in the shins. Stemple let go, and hopped about against the pain. He was furious himself now. 'You're as mad as your bloody mother,' he said.

'What?' demanded Mick.

'You belong in the bloody loony bin, like your bloody mad mother,' said Stemple.

Just then Betty emerged from the front door of the homestead, and looked around, calling, 'Mick! Mick! Where are you?'

'Better get back,' said Stemple, forcing himself to calm down. He turned and bent over his task, returning to the work of cleaning out Willy's trough.

Then Mick did something he was to be ashamed of for the rest of his life. He took his pencil, raised his arm high, and stabbed it violently into Stemple's back, just below the left shoulder blade. It was a pencil that had been freshly sharpened. It made a horrible crunching noise as it went in, and snapped in half, leaving a ragged stump embedded in Stemple's back.

Stemple bellowed, and Mick threw the broken pencil down and took to his heels before Stemple had even had a chance to turn round. He ran in a kind of wild panic to the shed where his motorcycle was kept, kicked it into life, and disappeared up the track in a cloud of red dust. He knew deep in his guts that he would never be able to go back and face the shame.

Mick sat with his arms around his knees in the darkness of the sacred cave, miserable beyond any misery he had experienced before. He was still trembling. He was thinking that if only he could get that white shard of quartz out of the water, it would be like a magic wand, and he could get rid of Stemple, and make Betty love him, and bring back his father, and make his mother better, and make everybody forget the vile thing he had just done.

He didn't have his torch with him, but he crept to the edge of the water, and reached down into it. It felt very silky and cold. He could not reach the stone, so he stretched ever further, and further, until he was in danger of falling in. He only just managed to save himself, and at that moment, right outside the cave, the strangest thing happened. There was a roaring noise. Mick scrambled out into the daylight and was almost plucked into the air. It was the kind of mini tornado that the locals called a Cock-Eyed Bob. Before his eyes it uprooted a gum tree and carried it up and away. The Cock-Eyed Bob travelled away in the direction of the river, and Mick watched it go, until it released the tree, which hit the ground like a man with a parachute, landing on its root ball and toppling over. Mick felt as though he had been taken out of the real world and cast into hell. His brains seemed to thud in his skull and beat against his temples. He returned to the cave, and sat there, becoming hungrier and sadder with every passing moment.

Three hours later he was asleep when Blue hurtled in through the entrance and leapt on him, covering him with slobbery kisses. Then he heard Granpa's voice. 'Come on out, boy. I know you're in there.'

Mick emerged into the blinding light, and Granpa looked him up and down and said, 'It's damn lucky we had that dog to find you. You get on that bike and get back home right now, understand?'

Mick rode back to the homestead with Blue sitting in front of him, and terror in his heart. He had never seen anyone so icy with anger as Granpa was. Granpa could probably have killed him with just one basilisk glance. Mick felt so sick in the stomach that it hurt.

He was sent to his room, and shortly afterwards Granpa appeared with Stemple at his side. Stemple was pale, and Granpa was still shaking with rage. He drew his belt from its loops, and handed it to Stemple. 'You've got the right to thrash him,' he said, and left the room.

Stemple stood there with Granpa's belt in his right hand, and faced Mick. Mick gazed back, unable to take his eyes away, and his lips trembled. Two huge tears ran down his cheeks, and his shoulders began to shake. He couldn't take his eyes off Stemple. This time he would not try to run away or escape. He imagined what the stroke of the belt would be like, the whistle of it as it whipped through the air, but knew that he deserved it, and he wasn't going to avoid it. Stemple stood there and looked back at him, weighing the belt in his hands.

Mick felt all the sadness and horror of the universe overwhelm him. His father was dead, his mother was in a home, he had made his grandfather ashamed of him, Betty would probably resign and leave, and he had stabbed a good man when his back was turned. He closed his eyes and stood to attention for a very long time, like a soldier on parade, awaiting the lash, tears pouring down his face. He was so afflicted with grief that it was difficult to remain upright at all.

Finally there was a movement, and Mick flinched, but then he felt strong arms around him, and a kind voice in his ear saying softly, 'Sometimes it's a sin to love too much, mate.'

Stemple knelt there hugging him and stroking his hair. Stemple smelled of timber, sweat, sunshine, horses and engine oil. For Mick it brought back memories of his father after a day's work at the weekend, and he relaxed into the embrace, putting his arms around Stemple, and burying his head in his shoulder. Stemple's body felt as though it were made of rock.

After an age, Mick calmed down and stopped sobbing. At last Stemple released him, stood up and handed him the belt, saying, 'Here, now it's your turn. Give me a swipe.'

Mick looked at him uncomprehendingly. 'Go on, land me one …' Stemple paused '… for what I said about your mum.'

Mick knew he could not possibly hit Stemple. He just let the belt hang by his side.

'I was out of order,' said Stemple. 'I apologise. It was mean. You know I'm not … I'm not normally mean like that.'

'And I'm sorry. For stabbing you with the pencil.'

Stemple looked into the crumpled face of the troubled and grief-stricken little boy. 'Shake,' he said, holding out his hand, and they shook hands. Stemple put his arm around Mick's shoulder and said, 'You'd better give that belt back to your grandad. We wouldn't want him to drop his strides, would we?'

That night Mick dreamed that he was drowning in the sacred pool. In the early hours there was a lightning storm, and poor Willy the mad one-eyed thoroughbred was struck for a second time, and was dead under the poinciana tree by the morning. Mick found him when he went out to breathe in his nostrils, as he did every day before breakfast. He ran to fetch his grandfather, and they knelt by the horse's body, just looking at it.

For Granpa it was like losing a connection with long-lost golden days. 'D'you mind going back indoors?' he said to Mick, his voice breaking, and the boy stood up and walked away. He sat on a chair on the terrace, just able to see his grieving grandfather crouched down in the long brown grass, with his head laid on the horse's neck.

For some reason Mick took all this as a sign that he should never go in the magic cave again.

THE FLAMES

Mick came into the schoolroom one morning and found Betty sitting by the radio with her face in her hands, crying. He didn't know what to do, except stand beside her and put his hand on her shoulder. Betty looked up, said, 'Oh Mick!', put her arms around him, and hugged him to her. After his attack on Stemple, Betty had treated him with frosty professionalism, and he had never expected her to be nice to him again. This sudden affection was a surprise.

'Why are you crying?' he asked, expecting her to say that Stemple had been horrible to her.

'I'm such a blubberguts,' she said, 'I can't help it.' She wiped her eyes on a small handkerchief, and said, 'I'm going to miss you so much. I'm going to miss everybody.

I'm sorry, I know I shouldn't cry like this. I should be happy for you.'

'Miss me? But who's going to teach me?'

'Teach you? Why, haven't you heard?'

'Heard what?'

'You're going to Melbourne.'

'Melbourne?' Mick was astonished and frightened. He'd never been to Melbourne. What on earth was he going to do there?

'Your mum, she's turned up in Melbourne. She's told your grandad she wants you back.'

'Is she better then?' asked Mick, not quite sure what to feel.

'I can't honestly say, Micko. I hope she is, I really do.'

'Who's going to teach me?'

'You're going to Melbourne Grammar. And you're going to be a boarder, at least till your mum really can cope.'

'Boarding school? I don't want to go! What about Blue? What about Lamington?'

'There's no way your grandad'd let you take the cat,' said Betty, laughing through her tears.

Neither Betty nor Mick could concentrate on lessons that morning, so Betty let him out early. He found his grandfather adjusting the drive on the wind pump, and stood quietly, waiting for him to finish.

'I s'pose you heard then,' said Granpa.

'I don't want to go,' said Mick.

'I don't want you to go, either.'

'Why have I got to go then?'

'Your mother.'

'Why can't she come here?'

'I did ask her. She's a city girl, Mick. She's landed herself a job part-time. She's on the mend, she wants her little boy back. What would she do round here, anyway?'

'I don't want to!'

Granpa sighed. 'Listen, son, life isn't always about what you want. It's not even often. More often than not it's about doing what's best. Doing your duty. I've looked after you while I had to, and you know what? I loved every minute of it, and I'm going to miss you like copper-bottomed hell. I want to be frank with you, all right?'

Mick nodded dumbly, looking up into his grand-father's weather-beaten face and startlingly blue eyes.

'When you go to Melbourne it'll be more like you looking after your mum than her looking after you. D'you catch my drift? She needs you there, steady like a rock, to lead her out. And you'll do it because you love her, like I love you.'

'What about Blue?'

Granpa put his hand on Mick's shoulder. 'It wouldn't be kind, would it? Blue's a bush dog. He trots for miles on his own. He goes out for adventures. He gets into shindigs with perenties and dingos. What's he going to do in Melbourne except get into trouble and croak from boredom? I'll take good care of him, and you can come back as often as you like, and he won't have forgotten you, and it'll always be like old times. You'll always have a home here, son, just like your dad always did.'

'I'm not going,' said Mick. 'I'm going to take Blue, and go and be an outlaw. Like Ned Kelly.'

'Kelly got shot 'cause he was too stupid to make the rest of his suit of armour.'

'I'm taking Blue and I'm going.'

'Well, best of luck, mate.' Granpa held out his hand, and said, 'Shake. I wish you all the best, I really do. What are you going to do when you run out of gas?'

Mick ignored the question, and went to the kitchen, where he made a real pigsnout sandwich, with Vegemite, ham, tomatoes and marmalade. He filled a bottle with water and went to check that the tank of his bike was full.

He called Blue. Together they rode out of the homestead, with Mick wondering whether to go to Roebourne or Cossack before beginning his life of outlawry. He chose the latter, and arrived just as Sergeant Sam was tossing a heap of crabs into a big saucepan in order to make crab soup.

'G'day,' said Sam. 'What might you be after?'

'I'm running away,' replied Mick, 'and so's Blue.'

'Where to?'

'I thought I could live here. At first, anyway. I'm going to go bush, and learn how to live on bush tucker from the blackfellas.'

118

Sam frowned. 'You can't stay here, mate. It's too crowded already. And the bush blackfellas have all gone. Got turned into jackaroos, and now they're in Roebourne with bugger all to do.'

'But it's just you here. And those Greeks with the fishing boat.'

'Exactly. Too bloody crowded. You'll have to go somewhere else. It's not that I don't like you. I just don't like company.'

'I'll leave you alone.'

'Well, that wouldn't be very nice, would it?'

'Can I just stay for a while?'

'Stay and have some of this crab soup. It'll be bonzer when it's done.'

'I've got a sandwich.'

'We'll go halves. What's in the sandwich?'

'Vegemite, marmalade, ham and tomatoes.'

'Blimey, mate.'

The soup wasn't bad, but the sandwich was pretty weird, and Sam gave some of his to Blue, who wolfed it down in a second.

'That dog's a hell of a gutbucket,' said Sam, and then he looked up and noticed something. He pointed into the distance. 'Isn't your grandad's place over there? That's Regal Ridge, isn't it?'

Mick looked where Sam was pointing, and saw a pall of black smoke rising into the sky.

Mick was horrified. He knew which way the wind was blowing, and the implications were both clear and terrible. He had no choice, and he knew it. This was no time to be running away and dreaming of being an outlaw, and it wasn't just a question of love, it was a question of personal honour. He got back on his bike, kicked it over, and Blue scrambled up in front of him, putting his paws on the handlebars. With fear thudding in his guts, Mick drove back home.

It became more and more difficult and frightening, the closer he came to the homestead. He stopped and wondered if he could possibly make it through. Then he kicked the bike into gear and let out the clutch, remembering where the track went, and knowing that for a few seconds he would probably be blinded by the smoke. He was strangely reassured by Blue's presence, and could hardly believe his own bravery as he entered the swirling inferno, a courage raised up in his heart by the desperate love he felt for those on the other side of the flames.

He only just made it through the resinous smoke and the horrible flying cinders that somehow got between his clothing and his flesh, and stung him with tiny burns. The eucalypts burned with ferocious heat, as if presoaked in petrol, and seemed to send up their own individual tornadoes. As terrifying as the heat and smoke was the roaring and crackling of the flames, and the exploding of trees as they split apart. It sounded like gunshots.

At the homestead, all the hands, including Betty, were concentrating on the only thing that mattered, which was to protect the buildings. Granpa was an experienced man, and many years before he had learned the hard way that you have to have a firebreak around your house. His was a circle of treeless and shrubless ground a hundred yards deep, with nothing but scrubby grass growing in it. You let the fire take the grass, which burns away very quickly, and then you patrol constantly to put out any flame that sets itself up anywhere near the house.

Granpa and the crew were armed with hessian sacks that contained sodden oats, and when Mick arrived, Granpa just nodded to him and pointed to where the supply of wet sacks lay, by the water tower, where Taylor Pete was replenishing them. Mick sent Blue into the house, and shut the door.

They fought the fires all day.

Mick had never been so hot and thirsty in his life. He felt as though he had been breathing flames, and his lungs ached inside his chest. From head to foot he became as black as Taylor Pete, and Taylor Pete became even blacker than himself. They all looked like devils from hell, with wild eyes staring out from their faces, and you could hardly tell who was Stemple, who was Betty, and who was Granpa. At the water tower they took cups of water, gulped them down, and then poured more cups over their heads and clothes. You had to keep yourself soaked.

The dreadful ordeal only ended in the early evening, when the wind quite suddenly changed and drove the

121

fire back upon itself. The people found themselves looking out over a desolate landscape of blackened stumps, with a great cloud of black smoke hanging above it like a scene from some apocalyptic battlefield.

Granpa came and stood beside Mick, who was leaning on a rake, begrimed from head to foot, and utterly exhausted. 'You should have seen yourself turning up on that bike between the walls of smoke,' said Granpa. 'It was like something from a movie. Like bloody Steve McQueen.' Then he gestured at the blackened and smoking land, and said, 'You may not believe this, son, but all that's damned good for the farm. That's how mother nature feeds herself. You missed something pretty wonderful, though.'

'What did I miss?'

'The animals. They came charging past. The roos, the wallabies, you'd never think we had so many of 'em. And that perentie, the one that gave you that weal, he came rushing by on his hind legs like he was going for a medal.'

'I'm sorry I ran away, Granpa.'

'Hell,' replied Granpa, 'everyone runs away, son. It's how we return that means something. You couldn't have improved on that.'

DUST ON HIS KNEES

Betty and Stemple left the day before Mick did, in Stemple's ute. They were going to take the great coastal highway down to Perth, and there they were going to set about their scheme for getting on the road as musicians. It would be a long but beautiful drive, and they'd be taking turns at the wheel, talking about the years to come, dreaming aloud of travelling all over Australia with their vanload of amplifiers and instruments, playing in bars and clubs, and then at concert halls and festivals, until one day they would be sending their gear off in a truck while they travelled in planes. As they drove away from that Martian landscape, there was not one moment when they doubted their destiny.

Mick wrote Betty a little note, saying, *Dear Betty,*

Thank you for all the education. Mick, and left it on her bed.

When Betty found it, she came out and hugged him tearfully. It was lovely to smell her scent of lavender again. She said, 'I want to tell you something. Just between you and me. Promise you won't pass it on?'

Mick nodded.

'Promise with silver bells and pink ribbons? Promise, promise, promise?'

He nodded again, and Betty whispered, 'If you'd been a few years older, Stemple wouldn't have stood a chance. I'd have chosen you any day. You know that, don't you?'

Mick had not known it, but he felt his heart lift.

'It's not your fault being young,' said Betty, 'it's my fault being old.'

She stood up and kissed him on the forehead, saying, 'You're my ideal man, you are.'

And for many years to come, Betty remained Mick's ideal woman.

Later on, Stemple said to Mick, 'Thanks for the scar, mate. Every man needs a scar left over from fighting over a good woman. You did me a favour.'

Betty and Stemple departed in a tall plume of dust, tooting their horn and waving out of the windows, on their long journey into the future. That evening Jimmy Umbrella cooked up garfish so that Mick could have the pleasure of the green bones for the last time, and afterwards he took the bones and fried them up

124

until they were deliciously crisp, so Mick and his grandfather could crunch their way through them. At the end of the meal, Granpa gave Mick his first little tot of Bundy and said, 'Don't tell your mum.' It burned its way down Mick's throat and into his stomach, and he felt a little strange almost straight away. For a moment it seemed that he was a man, in companionable silence with another man.

'You've always got a home here, son,' said Granpa. 'You remember that. See if you can bring your mum out here sometime. It might help. I'll make sure that Taylor Pete keeps the bike running. And by the way, I've got no one else to leave this station to. I don't know if you're interested. Think about it.' He looked away and added, 'The quack thinks I've got a bad ticker.'

At bedtime Granpa stood up and went to fetch something, and gave it to Mick. It was very badly wrapped, so Mick knew his grandfather had done it. Mick tore the paper off, and found Tom Quilty's *The Drover's Cook and Other Verses*.

'When you read that, try and imagine me reading it,' said Granpa. 'That's how I want you to remember me.'

On the flyleaf was written: *To My Best Mate Mick, With Love and Thanks, Granpa.*

On the morning of his departure, just after dawn, Mick went for his last walk with Blue, to the place where he had found his first petroglyph, that day so many months ago when he had gone out looking for snakes, armed only with Granpa's rhyme. As he scrambled up among the rocks, he noticed something hanging in a bush that looked curiously familiar. He laughed with amazement and delight, and went to collect it, turning it over in his hands, smiling, and putting it over his head to make Blue bark. It was very bleached by the sun, and there was a crack on one side, but it was nothing that Taylor Pete couldn't mend.

When Mick got home he presented it to his grandfather, who said, 'My word! You found that?' He took it from his grandson and laughed. 'I've been missing this, even though we got a new one. This is the real thing, this is. Thanks, son.'

It was the wooden seat from the dunny, which had been whirled away by the cyclone.

Mick said goodbye to Lamington, and the horses, and the small black pigs, and the chooks, and to Blue, who sensed Mick's sadness, and consented to sit still on the veranda with Mick's arm around him until the plane arrived.

Dressed in his best and only suit, with the roo's toe bone in his trouser pocket, Mick made his way with Blue, Taylor Pete and Grandad to the makeshift landing strip. Pete insisted on carrying Mick's case, which contained only a few clothes, his roo's femur and his torch. Granpa had asked him to leave his cricket bat behind, so that they would have one when he came back. When the droning of the little Cessna was heard in the distance, Taylor Pete took a small bag out of his pocket, closed with a drawstring. 'Here, mate,' was all he said. Mick opened it and peered in. It contained a small red rock and a handful of red earth. Mick closed the pouch up again and put it in his pocket.

Pete bent down and scooped up some red dust. 'Put your hands out, mate,' he said, and he meticulously rubbed the dust into Mick's palms, and in between the fingers. 'No escape now,' he said.

Mick was taken away by the same Cessna that had delivered him so long ago, piloted by the same crazy man, who came in to land, ran his wheels along the ground and then looped up before returning.

As the plane taxied to a halt beside them, Taylor Pete shook Mick's hand, and Granpa hugged him round the shoulder. Granpa said, 'Thanks for taming Willy. It's a shame he went. I'll get another thoroughbred for when you come back.'

The boy went down on his knees and put his arms around the dog's neck. Then, too numb to speak or to cry, dressed in his suit, with dust on his knees, and his hands stained red, Mick climbed into the aircraft, and left the Pilbara.

As the plane banked away in the direction of Port Hedland, Mick looked down and saw the homestead, and Taylor Pete and his grandfather still waving, becoming smaller and smaller. Then he noticed a

127

dark-red spot hurtling along behind, in pursuit of the plane, kicking up a small trail of ochre dust in his wake.

Blue got as far as Cossack before he lost the last lingering scent of aviation fuel.

AFTERWORD

This book came about in a peculiar manner. After the success of the film of *Red Dog*, its producer, Nelson Woss, who was by now bonkers about red cloud kelpies, decided to make a prequel.

We know almost nothing about Red Dog before he became the Pilbara Wanderer, although we do know that he was originally called Blue. Nelson's film would necessarily be a fantasy. When it was in the can, it occurred to him that it might be a good idea to have it novelised so that a book could come out at the same time as the film, in 2016.

When the idea was suggested to me, I was very hostile to it, as I am far too grand and snobbish to turn other people's stories into novels, and in any case I was busy with an enormous trilogy. However, I then read the script, which I liked enormously, and decided that I was not too grand after all. Furthermore, I am almost as bonkers about Western Australia as Nelson is about red cloud kelpies, and I knew I would take pleasure in travelling back there, even if only in my imagination. Like *Red Dog*, this book was written for twelve-year-olds, and will probably be read mainly by adults.

Novelists are routinely appalled and dismayed by what scriptwriters and film directors do to their stories.

I have therefore been completely shameless about diverging from the script, excellent though it is, because revenge is sweet.

Louis de Bernières

GLOSSARY OF AUSTRALIANISMS

Anzac bickies: sweet biscuits popular in Australia and New Zealand.

Bandicoot: Australian marsupial, looks a little like a rat.

Barramundi: kind of fish.

Blue: violent dispute.

Boondocks: the middle of nowhere.

Boomer: large male kangaroo.

Brumby: wild horse.

Bull catcher: vehicle equipped with a large bull bar at the front.

Bunaga: this is a kinship term, relating to skin groups or moieties.

Bundy: Bundaberg rum, a popular Australian rum. Every Aussie gets horribly drunk on it at least once in a lifetime.

Bunyip: large creature from Aboriginal mythology that lurked in swamps and other waterways. It has entered mainstream Australian folklore.

Bush tucker: food sourced from the outback.

Daggy: ill-kempt.

Damper: crude bread made without yeast, much relied on by the early pioneers.

Dinkum: genuine, honest.

Dreamtime: the spiritual belief of Australian Aborigines about the origin of the Earth and its creation stories.

Drongo: slow-witted person.

Dugong: marine mammal that looks a bit like a seal.

Dunny: lavatory.

Esky: insulated plastic hamper for keeping food and drink cool when you are travelling.

Full as a goog: very drunk.

Galah: kind of cockatoo. Can also mean a fool or an idiot.

Garfish: long, thin fish, also known as a sea needle.

Goanna: kind of lizard. There are about 30 different species of goanna, and their length can be anything from 20 centimetres to 2.5 metres.

Going bush: disappearing on your own.

Gum trees: eucalyptus trees. Australia has an amazing number of different kinds.

Gwardar: kind of snake. Highly venomous.

Jackaroo: young man who works on a sheep or cattle station.

Libby's: company known for its tinned food.

Longneck: bottle of beer.

Maban: Aboriginal leader who is believed to have spiritual powers.

Mob: group of animals.

More front than Myer's: to be very confident. The phrase refers to Myer, a large department store in Melbourne with a wide shopfront.

Mulla mulla: species of plant that grows in abundance throughout the Pilbara.

Perentie: biggest Australian lizard; it can be up to 2.5 metres long.

Pigsnout sandwich: enormous sandwich suitable for a really greedy person.

Pilbara: mining region in Western Australia.

Poinciana tree: type of tree with vivid orange or scarlet flowers.

Red cloud kelpie: type of Australian sheepdog.

Sandgroper: someone from Western Australia.

Snaggers: sausages.

Spinifex: prickly undergrowth.

Station: rural property where sheep and cattle are raised.

Stiff bickies: bad luck.

Stubbie: small beer bottle.

Swagman: from Australian folklore, a person who travelled around the country on foot, carrying with him his personal belongings – his swag – usually wrapped in a bedroll.

Tinnie: can of beer.

Ute: pickup truck.

VoVos: kind of biscuit topped with raspberry jam and coconut.

Walkabout: whitefella term for a wander in the wilderness. Originally part of the initiation of young Aborigines.

Woop Woop: imaginary outback town a long way from anywhere.

Yakka: work.